PASSION—AT A PRICE

I could see in a flash how the plot would develop, what my own future would be. The short burst of an Indian summer, and then the long, slow, painful and shameful descent into the darkness. Jealousies, recrimination, humiliation, the grasping at straws. The complete disintegration of a character—just as it took place in my books. Was it really going to happen to me? Nonsense, I told myself firmly. I wanted some happiness and I was fully prepared to pay for it. It was a hard-headed bargain.

PLOT
COUNTER-PLOT

ANNA CLARKE

BERKLEY BOOKS, NEW YORK

PLOT COUNTER-PLOT

A Berkley Book / published by arrangement with
the author

PRINTING HISTORY
William Collins Sons & Co. Ltd. edition/June 1974
Charter edition/June 1990
Berkley edition / October 1990

ISBN: 0-425-12796-6

A BERKLEY BOOK ® TM 757,375
Berkley Books are published by The Berkley Publishing Group,
200 Madison Avenue, New York, New York 10016.
The name "BERKLEY" and the "B" logo
are trademarks belonging to Berkley Publishing Corporation.

PRINTED IN THE UNITED STATES OF AMERICA

10 9 8 7 6 5 4 3 2

PART ONE

PROLOGUE

At last I am alone in the room and can take up my pen to start the novel that may be the last one I shall ever write. I must work quickly and lose no time, for I must write in secret and everything I have written must be hidden from human eye. Jane Austen, it is said, slipped her manuscript sheets under the blotter to conceal them from the inquisitive glance of visiting acquaintances. My reason for concealment is more sinister.

I sit at the old roll-top desk where I have so often sat before, gazing out through the long balcony window across the promenade to the ever-moving expanse of the sea. The cars come by incessantly but do not disturb me; I am so used to them. Nor does inspiration fail; it is all there waiting to find release—a great simmering cauldron in my mind. Only the opportunity has been lacking. But now it has come and I am still too nervous to begin, not only for fear that somebody will return home too soon and catch me in the act, but also for fear of myself. For ever since I began to write it has haunted me, this fear that my imagination could take over my real life and that I could behave like one of the characters in my novels, even to the point of committing murder. It is murder that I am planning now, as I have done so many times to please innumerable readers. Only this time it is non-fiction; there will be a real corpse.

But perhaps when I have lived through it all again by writing it down I shall see some other solution. It is worth a try.

3

It ought not to be so hard to start. I know the formula well. I have used it eighteen times before—twenty times if you count the two unpublished typescripts that I put aside as an insurance against illness or lack of inspiration. The main character is a psychopathic personality, somebody of ability holding a responsible position, and I trace the disintegration of the personality from a little incident that triggers it off, right through to the final catastrophe. There are various minor characters to fill in the background and there is usually a "detached observer" type of character who takes the reader into his confidence and gives an intimate, gossipy air to the whole story. This person survives the holocaust at the end and leaves the reader with the reassuring feeling that there is, after all, still a normal life ready to be picked up again somewhere.

Which of the two am I? The character who is doomed? Or the one who survives? Even now I do not know the answer. Perhaps when I have finished writing I shall know at last.

— 1 —

The triggering incident came shortly after my fifty-first birthday, when my public reputation was at its height. I had made enough money to live luxuriously in this beautiful Regency house on Brighton seafront and I had no cause to worry that sickness might reduce my income. Nor was there much danger of failing inspiration, since my writing had become a compulsion. I was no more able to stop myself turning out books than the obsessional neurotic can prevent himself from endlessly washing his hands or going back to see whether he has switched off the light, or whatever else his particular kink might be.

I first started to write to escape from reality; to dull the pain of the final break with my lover. The cure was startlingly successful, but, like so many miracle drugs, it produced a different sort of disease—a sort of atrophy of the emotions, a feeling of being totally cut off from any genuine contact with other people. I lived in my books; I lived my characters' lives. And my most successful character creation of all was that of Helen Mitchell, novelist, formidable yet kindhearted, successful and yet curiously remote from the world. I created her without even knowing that I was doing it. It was many years after I had torn out my heart and—so I believed—thrown it away that I realized what a wretchedly shrivelled little personality was concealed beneath the Helen Mitchell shell. Shrivelled, but nonetheless dangerously alive. Try as we will to quench the fire of feeling, its ashes still smoulder on, ready to flare up again when least expected.

So it was with me.

On a Sunday evening towards the end of May I had invited about twenty people to celebrate the publication of the latest Helen Mitchell novel. Such gatherings had become obligatory; invitations were much sought after and a great deal of name-dropping and manoeuvring for status went on among the select company of authors, reviewers and other literary persons present. Helen Mitchell played her part with the nonchalance of long experience and after the last guest had gone she found herself standing alone in the big drawing-room on the first floor, staring into the gilt-framed mirror that hung over the great moulded mantelpiece.

Who are you, I thought, in your plain black dress—for to be timelessly elegant, outside fashion and trend, was part of the image—who are you with your smooth dark hair and your unwrinkled pale face and childish blue eyes. A non-face, non-person, stopped dead fifteen years ago, and operating since then purely as a word-spinning machine, keeping away pain and fear by turning out the product over and over again.

I stared and I wondered for longer than usual. Beneath the familiar fatigue of the evening there was a new and different sensation within me, a deep restlessness as of the sap miraculously rising in the roots of a long-withered tree. When, the better to suppress the revolt, I tried to trace its cause, my mind formed a picture of one of the guests who had been present—a young author who had produced one exceedingly successful novel but nothing more. I had met him several times and type-cast him as a shallow, charming, selfish and insincere young man. His star was already on the wane; he would probably not be invited to Helen Mitchell's next Sunday evening gathering.

Poor boy. I made a conscious effort to try to convert my restlessness into compassion—a permissible emotion—and my ever ready imagination gladly took up the task of presenting his image and his personal dilemma in neat, pithy phrases. That ought to have defused the bomb, but it didn't. The restlessness remained, together with a strong desire to talk to somebody about him. It was a very long time since I had experienced a wish of such urgency. It was in quite a different category from the irrational anxieties and the very mild satisfaction—usually more in the nature of relief from discomfort than of any positive joy—that had come to make up the emotional content of my life. I savoured to the full the rare and precious sensation of having something I really wanted to do, before I took any steps to gratify the wish. Then I went to the phone and pressed the knob that communicated with the ground floor where Mrs. Simmonds, my housekeeper, had her rooms.

"They're all gone," I said. "Shall we clear up now? Or would you rather leave it till tomorrow?"

"Let's do it now," she said.

While we washed up we talked about all the guests except the one who interested me most, and I continued to relish the joys of anticipation. It wasn't until we were relaxing over tea and a last cigarette that I mentioned his name.

"Brent Ashwood got very drunk after you went downstairs," I said, "and told everyone for the umpteenth time who the originals of all those women in his book were."

Mrs. Simmonds's somewhat protuberant eyes opened even wider.

"What do you think of him?" she asked.

"What do you?" I countered.

"Well, he's very good-looking, of course," she said, "and doesn't he just know it!"

"Such a dreadful name," I murmured. "Brent Ashwood. And his real one, apparently. Makes me think of a carpenter's shop."

"Or a London suburb in the wilds of Essex."

I laughed aloud. Mrs. Simmonds was a cheerful, good-natured soul and an extremely efficient housekeeper. She had been with me for five years and we had developed a pleasant enough companionship in little things, with each of us carefully observing the other's tastes and habits in matters of food and drink, hours of rest, and so on. She was a widow and had a married daughter with whom she spent her week-ends off duty. This family, I suspected, knew a lot more about me than I was ever told about them. Mrs. Simmonds obviously enjoyed having an insider's view of the literary world, and also an inside view of the Helen Mitchell character, and during our gossip sessions I could see her mentally storing up

tidbits to relate to her own people. I had a certain curiosity
to know how I myself figured in her narratives and was vain
enough to hope that the picture was one of an absent-minded
intellectual depending on her brisk, sensible housekeeper. At
times, however, I had a nasty suspicion that Mrs. Simmonds
presented a very different portrait of me—that of a lonely,
unhappy middle-aged woman, with many acquaintances but
few real friends, starved of love, cut off from life. Usually I
went to some trouble to emphasize the first portrait and blur
the edges of the second, but on this particular evening it did
not seem to matter what impression I gave: I just wanted talk
about Brent.

"Is he a good writer?" prompted Mrs. Simmonds.

"I'm afraid," I replied, "that he is very much a one-book
author and he is rapidly exhausting the capital—both money-
wise and publicity-wise—that accumulated from that one
book."

Mrs. Simmonds moved from the arm to the seat of the
settee and poured herself another cup of tea. I leaned back
in an armchair and began my monologue. Helen Mitchell—
cynicism laced with compassion, to quote a recent interview—was about to give her considered opinion.

"Brent Ashwood has written a novel about his mother, his
sister, his two ex-wives and three mistresses—quite an
achievement to have amassed all these by the age of twenty-
eight. In other words, he has written a novel about Brent
Ashwood. It has the requisite number of scenes of rape and/
or sexual humiliation, suitably spaced throughout the volume.
The language is also according to prescription and he has
been selected by his publishers for a special promotion cam-
paign, possibly by some random method but more likely because of his looks and because he can produce an impressive
list of totally irrelevant experiences—as tanker-driver, barman, life-guard, etc., including the obligatory spell in a
mental hospital. *Road Without End* is about an illegitimate
long-distance lorry driver who was "awakened" at an early
age by his mother and half-sister, and who subsequently does
very nicely on his own account. It has some entertaining dialogue now and then but is otherwise rather dull. It has sold
well both at home and abroad and is to be filmed. The author
has appeared in a television quiz programme and in a reli-

gious discussion and has given his opinion on a variety of subjects. The vital second novel has, however, yet to appear. I doubt whether it has even been started. Presumably the intention was to write a book about a barman who was "awakened" at an early age, etc. But something appears to have gone wrong. Hence the drinking. His best hope now would be to write a novel about a life-guard who writes a successful novel and is unable to cope with his fame. I should have liked to give him this advice, because I feel rather sorry for him, but unfortunately he was too drunk to take it in."

Mrs. Simmonds looked at me with some awe and asked:

"Don't you think he will write any more?"

"It doesn't look too hopeful at the moment."

"Then what will become of him?"

"He may become an alcoholic—unless his current woman manages to keep him off it. Or have a mental breakdown."

"But that's terrible." Mrs. Simmonds looked really distressed. "Wouldn't it have been better for him if he had never had the book published at all?"

"I don't know," I said thoughtfully. "He has got some talent. And if he *can* get over this crisis he might just possibly produce something better. Occasionally it happens that way."

I drifted off into generalizations. Caution had reasserted itself and told me to stop talking about Brent. Mrs. Simmonds listened politely for a few minutes, then she yawned, got up and drew a curtain aside, and said:

"Moonlight over the sea. It's a lovely night."

I joined her at the window and looked out across the promenade to the faint shimmer on the dark water beyond.

"You'd need to go right down on the beach, out of range of the illuminations," I said, "to get the full effect. Our manmade light spoils it from here."

A stupid, trite remark. I made it in order to cover up the sudden pain that had assailed me. It was not so much present emotion as a memory of past feeling. A torment of yearning, a blotting out of all the world in a blind, self-destructive craving to possess another person. How could there be such pain from such a very old wound? My mind sought phrases in which to describe it, pulled me back, unresisting, on to the treadmill of composition. Words came flowing—scenes, characters, dialogue—and drove away the sharp memory of grief.

But still the restlessness remained. Long after Mrs. Simmonds had gone to bed I lingered on the balcony, with the big room in darkness behind me, watching the young couples strolling along the promenade—dirty jeans and torn tunics entwined together, straggling dark hair falling over straggling fair hair, faces pale, unsmiling, spotted with acne. Thus my mind described them. But their minds were engaged on imagination's rightful task—to transform the commonplace into the unique, to beautify the unlovely, to build on a firm foundation of real life and not to corrode life, eat it away like a cancer.

I dissected them with my words and yet I envied them. Weighed down though each might be with his own burden of circumstances, yet each one was vibrantly alive. They had other human beings to love and hate, quarrel with, worry about, talk about, plan for. I balanced their lives against my own splendid isolation of wealth and fame and I thought: could I make a pact with the devil I would offer all I possess, gladly throwing in this word-spinning facility of mine, in return for one short episode of real human contact. And then I smiled at myself. That would be the next novel—a modern Faust, a female one. I had deceived myself yet again. This miraculous upsurge of feeling, this sharply remembered pain—it was nothing but a new book stirring; it was no herald of a renewal of real life.

I went to bed at last, swallowed sleeping-pills, and lay fighting the flow of words in my mind. I didn't want to write this book. It was as if, having glimpsed the sun, I had been forced back into the feeble rays of a lamp. There was no joy in this creation, no rest from it save in the oblivion of sleep.

2

Mrs. Simmonds put the tray on the bedside-table and drew my curtains back a couple of inches so that I could gradually accustom myself to the bright morning light. When she had gone I poured a cup of tea and lay thinking about the day ahead. There were some proofs to be sent off and a few letters to write and a television serial that I intended to watch that evening. Not much to occupy sixteen hours of consciousness, and the rest of the time I would be compulsively word-spinning, either on paper or in my mind.

It looked like being another brilliant day, with the sea flashing and sparkling in the sunlight and the air caressingly mild. Yet here I was, with wealth and leisure and physical strength, shut up like a prisoner in my beautiful Regency house, for in recent years I had suffered intermittently from agoraphobia—the fear of being away from the safety of home—and today, I knew instinctively, was going to be a bad one. I would have to sit on the balcony and pretend to Mrs. Simmonds that I was too tired to go out, for to confess my weakness was out of the question. At times my fictional ingenuity was stretched to the limit to provide acceptable excuses for not doing the things I was afraid to do, but I preferred to be thought proud, unapproachable or obstinate, rather than have the truth revealed. And yet it was a common enough complaint, and to have admitted it would have been to take one little step towards freeing myself from the strait-jacket of my reputation in which I was confined.

The telephone rang and I picked up the receiver on the extension by my bed.

"Yes?" I smothered a yawn.

The possible callers flashed in speedy succession through my mind—my brother Philip, my friend Marian, my agent, the few dozen acquaintances to whom I had given my ex-directory number—nothing but tedium to be expected from a conversation with any of these. And yet in the same flash of thought I was excitedly expectant, convinced that this caller was not among those listed.

"Can I speak to Miss Mitchell, please?" said a man's voice carefully.

A faint accent. Might have been lapsed Cockney, or cultivated Australian, or acquired mid-Atlantic. I knew at once who it was, but the habit of defense was too strong to let me admit it.

"Speaking," I said abruptly. "Who is that?"

"Oh lord, is it you? I didn't expect to get straight through. Have I woken you up or something awful?"

"Who is it, please?" I repeated.

"It's Brent. I say, you weren't asleep, were you?"

"Brent?" My voice remained very cool. It was cheek of him to ring me. He barely warranted an invitation to a publication party; he was in no sense a personal friend and we were certainly not on chatty telephone conversation terms.

"Brent Ashwood." A slight pause, and then: "Please, Miss Mitchell, don't say the name means nothing to you! You did invite me to your party last night—honestly you did. I've still got the card—it's stuck up in a prominent place in my room—not that anyone comes to see me now who it's worth trying to impress."

I made a face and with difficulty restrained myself from correcting his grammar. The faint whining of self-pity in his last remark jarred on me and the clumsy flattery was no less offensive. And yet I was conscious of a quickening of interest, a sudden dispersal of my irrational anxieties, and a feeling that the day was not going to be so dreary after all.

"What do you want, Mr. Ashwood?" I asked.

"Lots of things. Sorry—there I go again. Why I'm really phoning you—and I know it's a liberty but I've been up for hours worrying about it and simply couldn't bear to wait any longer—is to apologize for my behaviour last night. It was unforgivable. Please forgive me.''

"I didn't notice anything particularly reprehensible about your behaviour," I said. "Parties are meant to be uninhibited occasions."

Again there was a slight pause. My reply seemed to have disconcerted him. Probably I had been intended to say "There's nothing to forgive," which would have resulted in repeated apologies, or, better still, I should have made some personal comment that would have given him an opening to launch forth about himself.

"It was a good party," he said, "and I only hope I didn't spoil it."

"No, indeed. I was glad you were able to come."

Stumped again. I could sense his frustration at the other end of the line. It was clear that he was trying to put our casual relationship on to a more intimate footing. It was not the first time that I had been the object of such an attempt and usually I had no difficulty in achieving the necessary degree of polite discouragement. I could have done so now but was curious to see what tactics he would employ next.

Or so I explained the matter to myself.

He laughed, apparently in genuine amusement, and said with calculated impudence: "I was warned you'd be tough going."

"Indeed?"

"That's the wrong answer, Miss Mitchell. You're meant to ask who warned me, and that leads on to a slanderous conversation about our mutual acquaintances."

"Indeed," I said again, but it hadn't quite the cool force of the first time. I was weakening; our roles had shifted and he was beginning to make the running. It would be difficult to get rid of him now without open rudeness. And his next words made any slick dismissal right out of the question.

"Oh, can't we cut out these preliminaries!" he cried impulsively. "I'm just about at the end and I'm sure you can help me and I'd like to come and see you. Very soon. Some time today?"

I said nothing. He would probably believe it if I said I was too busy, since nobody had any idea how uneventful my life really was. They seemed to think that I spent hours and hours pacing up and down the room in an agony of creative effort, that every book required hours more of talking to agents, publishers, and what-have-you, and that in whatever time was left I was warding off hundreds of invitations to broadcast, open bazaars, and so on. Suddenly I found myself longing to break through the pretense. I wanted this boy to come and see me, however uncongenial I might find his company. I wanted him to come in the same way as I had wanted to talk about him yesterday evening. It was a genuine wish and it filled me with elation. But in this case I could not take the initiative; I had to leave it to him, and I could only hope that he would find a way to make it impossible for me to refuse.

"I don't make a habit of forcing myself on busy people like this," he went on, since I had still made no reply, "but I'm so desperate that it seemed worth a try. You can't do worse than say no."

"Four o'clock," I said. "I'll expect you then. Don't make it any earlier."

He became effusive.

"Goodbye," I said firmly.

I replaced the receiver, took a drink of my now lukewarm tea, and inspected my reactions. The first was to wonder whether Mrs. Simmonds had been listening in on the other extension. It didn't matter; I had said nothing out of character, and such indiscretion as there was, was in my own consciousness alone. And there it must remain. To me it was a phenomenon both wonderful and alarming—this thawing out of the long-frozen capacity to respond; but to other people it would appear pitiable and ludicrous—a middle-aged woman falling in love with a man scarcely half her age. It was the sort of situation I could handle in a novel, that I was in fact thinking of using for my next book. It would be the mixture as before, the usual formula, although I had never before dared to come so near to basing the main character on myself. I had avoided this because it would awaken too many memories, and besides, there were other reasons why I could not bring into a book the experiences of my own life. I would have to be extremely careful if I used them now. But use them I must. This intense feeling of excitement must be a new book stirring; it could not possibly be anything else. A successful woman with a heart of stone—an artist perhaps, not a writer. All well on the surface, but with the seeds of a breakdown within, just waiting to be watered. A slow, inexorable collapse of personality that would lead to murder. And all set in motion by the telephone call from a comparative stranger. Totally unexpected.

But was it so unexpected? Had I made it happen? I could make it happen in my books. Which one was my heroine? Which one was myself.

For a few nightmarish moments I seemed to be teetering on a tightrope over a deep abyss. And then I picked up the pen and notebook that lay always by my bed. At this stage of a book my creatures would usually take control and I would write as if in a trance. My hand hovered over the page but no words came.

The flood had dried up; the treadmill had ground to a halt at last.

I remained for some time with the pen in my hand, unable to believe it. And then I put the pen and pad aside and forced myself to take stock of the situation. Some great change was taking place within me; the shrivelled creature inside the shell was coming to life and breaking out, and I did not know what it was going to do. Until I did know it would be best to keep up the pretense, to act my Helen Mitchell self. Mrs. Simmonds's arrival would be my first test; I should soon find out if she had noticed any difference in me.

"I must be losing my touch," I said laughingly to her when she came to collect the tray. "I've let Mr. Ashwood invite himself to tea today."

"Oh." Her reaction was markedly cool. "Is he to have the VIP treatment?"

"Yes, I think so. If we treat him informally as one of the family then he will think he's always welcome and we'll never get rid of him."

"Oh," she said again. And then a moment later: "Yes, I see what you mean."

"Anyway, it's time we had the silver out. We've not used it since the girl came to write us up for that new women's magazine."

Mrs. Simmonds clearly didn't like my inviting Brent to tea, and I hoped that she would be placated by my putting him in the same category as a newspaper reporter. She was a great observer of nice social distinctions. The ruse appeared to work. She smiled quite naturally and entered with enthusiasm into a discussion of domestic details.

"God knows what he wants," I said several times, hoping I was not overdoing the pretence at reluctance. "Unless it's to borrow money."

"Oh, Miss Mitchell, don't go doing that again!" Mrs. Simmonds looked quite upset. "You're much too generous. You shouldn't let these young scroungers get away with it, really you shouldn't. You've had to work hard. Why shouldn't they?"

"It's good publicity," I said, laughing, "and I don't miss a hundred pounds here and there."

But she wasn't convinced. "I don't like to see you taken in," she said, her face going redder and redder as it always did when she felt strongly about something, "and I wish you had somebody to look after you."

She stumped out of the room, leaving me surprised and thoughtful. In all the time she had been with me Mrs. Simmonds had never revealed so much of her own attitude towards me. It could surely only be in response to some change in myself. Of course I had said nothing to her about the feelings that had been stirring in me since last night, and she knew nothing about my past emotional life. And yet something had communicated itself to her. I would have to be even more on my guard. The last thing I wanted was to get tangled up in a personal relationship with Mrs. Simmonds. But with anybody else? It came into my mind that Mrs. Simmonds would be a most inconvenient person to have in the house if one was wanting to conduct an affair, and it suddenly became of great importance to work out a plan to keep her in the dark.

All the time I was eating breakfast, sitting by the long window opening on to the balcony and looking out at the glittering morning, my mind was occupied with the problem of circumventing Mrs. Simmonds. I gave it the sort of detached, yet faintly anxious concentration that I was accustomed to give to the mechanics of a plot, but I deliberately put no name nor face upon the supposed lover, nor was there, as yet, any element of day-dreaming present. I pretended, even to myself, that I was planning a book, pretended that I was completely in control. But underneath this I knew that I was no longer in control, that I had to wait to see what would happen. It was exciting and frightening both at the same time.

After breakfast I settled down to correcting proofs, working hastily, for the day that had felt so empty and endless seemed to have telescoped and I was afraid that I would not complete the few tasks I had set myself before my guest arrived. But by mid-day I had finished and there were still four hours to kill. I parcelled up the proofs and took them round to the sub-post office in the little shopping street that runs up from the seafront at the side of our terrace. The white-haired ex-schoolmaster who had recently taken over the shop and post office greeted me warmly:

"Morning, Miss Mitchell. Another masterpiece of mystery to tickle our fancy, would it be?"

I smirked at him. "For the Christmas trade. And how's business with you, Mr. Evans?"

He took the package and then leaned across the counter in a confiding manner:

"Two *New Statesman*'s and three *Listener*'s this morning. We're coming on. We'll raise the literary standards of this neighborhood yet."

"Well done," I said.

Normally at this point I would have left the shop, but today I felt an impulse to stay and chat. It was a sort of test, to see whether somebody with whom I had an amicable, skin-deep relationship was also aware of the change in me.

"Aren't the Regency Terrace dwellers great buyers of glossies and quality weeklies?" I asked. "I should have thought they would be."

Those were the words I uttered as I continued to beam at him, but what I really meant was: am not I, Helen Mitchell of the formidable image, still capable of arousing men's interest and admiration and perhaps even desire? Even a nice little elderly Welshman, with a beady little wife and a grown-up grandchild, would be capable of telling me that. But not in words, of course.

"Ah," said Mr. Evans, shaking his head at me, "you forget you are only a minority, you elegant sea-fronters. Just look at the great plebeian hinterland."

"I'm ashamed to say," I replied, "that I have scarcely ever looked at it."

It was on the tip of my tongue to admit to my phobia, but I was diverted by Mr. Evans's next remark.

"You ought to go exploring," he said. "There's some interesting old buildings around here."

And he launched forth into a catalogue of churches, pubs, and so on. Whether this could be considered an affirmative answer to my question I could not tell, but his enthusiasm did inspire me, when another customer came in and I made my escape, to brave the strange streets and try out my newfound confidence. I wandered about, amazed at the disappearance of the dark fears that I carried deep within me, delighted to be able to go into a greengrocer's shop and buy some apples just like everybody else. I found a church that Mr. Evans had mentioned and I peeped inside. I was a different being, strange to myself; a feeling creature, with a consciousness made up of all sorts of little hopes and expectations—irrational, shameful, stupid—not the poised and cynical Helen Mitchell at all.

But as I came out of the church I felt a familiar qualm: Who was I? What was I? Where was I?

I turned into a little alleyway in the direction of the sea. It was a cul-de-sac, ending in a blank wall. At the sight of this, panic struck. I swung round and ran blindly, tripping over uneven flagstones, letting my purchases fall to the ground. The church came once more into view. I ran up the road alongside. It led up a steep hill. This could not be right. I turned round again—a rat in a cage—seeing no way out. Everything was dim and whirling; faces came and went as in nightmare; leaden legs struggled and struggled but took me nowhere. And yet they must have moved because some time, many ages later, I was pushing the key into my own front door and calling out brightly to Mrs. Simmonds that I should be ready for lunch in ten minutes' time.

And then I sat in total hopelessness, cursing the false dawn that had led me into such an attack. Nothing was left of the excitement of the morning, of the renewed stirrings of life. It was all a feverish illusion; some virus must have gripped me. I was going to be ill, and I would have to put off this tiresome young man whom I had so longed to see.

I lifted the receiver and dialled his number; there was no reply. I tried again, and after Mrs. Simmonds had brought my lunch I rang once more, all to no avail.

I tried to write but no words came; I tried to read but the words made no sense. I said to myself again and again: you have been writing too much, this is a reaction of a tired brain that can create no longer; it has to fix itself on something and the something happens to be this boy. So I argued but I was not convinced. I was haunted by the sense of living in a story whose plot was completely determined, whose ending I could not escape.

At a few minutes to four I stepped out on to the balcony and
looked westwards towards the town. The broad busy roadway, the pier, the new tower blocks on the skyline—all looked
reassuringly solid and real, glowing in the light of common
day. The nightmarish feeling of lost identity had begun to
disperse and I could see myself playing the expected role. I
took my eyes off the distant view and focused them nearer—
on a spot just opposite where I stood. A man was leaning
against the railings of the promenade, not in the relaxed position of one staring mindlessly out to sea, but pressing himself against the rail and gripping it with both hands as if to
turn a somersault on to the lower walk fifty feet below. The
sun was so bright that it was difficult to distinguish colours,
but he seemed to be wearing a suit of pale blue or lilac, and
his fair hair lay in a heavy mane over the collar. His shoulders
were powerful but in the position in which he stood I could
not see his height.

He turned round and I felt myself give a little gasp. My
mind had given him the wrong face—not that of the young
author whom I scarcely knew, but that of another man, who
twenty-five years ago had been young and vigorous and fair.
Was there a likeness? I was too startled and confused to judge.
I drew back into the shadow of the window as the man standing on the promenade glanced up at the house. Then he looked
at his watch, stared around him with that lost and almost

desperate look that people so often have when they are alone, and stepped into the roadway.

I moved away from the balcony window, trembling, in my own elegant drawing-room, with the same kind of panic fear that earlier in the day had assailed me in the hostile streets. Was I having hallucinations? going mad? I had known perfectly well that Brent would shortly be arriving and yet I had, in some weird quirk of the mind, seen not his own features but those of Barry. Not Barry as he was now—rich, titled and famous—but as he had been when we first met: a bright working-class boy on the climb, teaching in a technical college, grabbing at every chance, using every possible means to shove himself forward. And always, looking wonderful. It was many years since I had allowed myself such a vivid flash of memory. The pain of it cleared my mind. Barry was dead to me. The man he was now knew nothing of the woman I was now. Helen Mitchell, successful novelist, was about to receive a young writer who was asking a favour. My Barry was dead. The past was dead, dead, dead.

The front doorbell rang. I moved to my roll-top desk which stood by the window, took up a pen, and tried to feel myself back into the part. There were footsteps on the stairs and a burst of laughter. I was suddenly annoyed: what right had Mrs. Simmonds to joke with one of my guests? The door was pushed open after a very perfunctory knock and Mrs. Simmonds came in, looking flushed and rather silly, as one caught out giggling over a primitive piece of humour. I looked at my irritation and found that it had its root in jealousy. Mrs. Simmonds was barely forty, and she had a tolerable face, and the sort of figure that looks as if it ought to be bursting out of some shiny material, behind a bar in a pub.

They were of the same world, she and the young man, and I was the outsider.

I got to my feet.

"Would you sit there," I said to Brent, "and perhaps you could bring tea straight away, Mrs. Simmonds. Then we shan't need to trouble you further if you want to go out."

"Certainly, Miss Mitchell." She recovered herself, rather overdoing the deference, and disappeared with evident relief into the kitchen. I turned my attention to Brent Ashwood, forcing myself to consider dispassionately whether he did bear any resemblance to Barry in his younger days. Yes, there was quite a marked likeness. My unconscious mind must have responded to it, while my conscious mind had not wanted to know. I had not noticed the resemblance before. Perhaps it was because Brent looked cleaner and tidier now than at last night's party or on the previous occasions when we had met. Barry had always been rather fastidious about his appearance and I had loved him all the more for it.

I passed a hand over my eyes; Barry had nothing whatever to do with the present interview. I must attend to the moment and forget the past.

"Do you want to ask me about it now, or shall we have tea first?" I said.

"Ask you?" Brent looked genuinely puzzled.

"You have a request to make. You rang up this morning and said you were in a terrible mess and only I could help you."

"Oh yes."

He still sounded vague. He was twisting about as though unable to find a satisfactory position in the very comfortable armchair, and looking restlessly around the big room—at the bookshelves, the gilt-framed mirror, the oval table and chairs near the inner wall, and at my desk. In fact at everything except at me.

"The room looks different," he said almost angrily.

"Rooms always do during the day, and when they're not full of people."

"And you look different too."

This startled me. I could not reply; I could only try to appear aloof.

"You must think I've got an awful cheek," he said next.

The old-fashioned schoolboy phrase came oddly from his lips. Had he rehearsed this scene, or was he really ill at ease?

"Not at all," I said.

He twisted about again, his eyes finally coming to rest once more on the desk. I answered his unspoken question.

"It belonged to my father. He was an Anglican vicar. This stood in his study for many years."

"Do you work at it or is it just for show?"

"A bit of both."

There was a silence. Normally, when people were as nervous as he was, I would help them out, but I was still very much thrown off balance by all the sensations and fears and memories that had been crowding in upon me since the previous evening and had no certainty that I would be able to keep up my role.

"Do you write for so many hours every day?" he next wanted to know.

The stock question of the interviewer; I had heard it many times and it gave me back some confidence.

"Mr. Ashwood, if you really want an account of my working habits you will find one in the current issue of *Woman's Monthly*, which is no more of a travesty than any of the other so-called portraits."

He looked scared for a moment, then his features relaxed into a grin and he brought his hands together silently, miming applause.

"Vintage Helen Mitchell! *Now* I'm beginning to feel better."

But I'm not, I thought as Mrs. Simmonds brought in the tea-trolley. This appeared to be his technique: extreme gaucherie, which provoked one into a sharp retort that gave him an opening to step on to a more personal plane. A week ago, even two days ago, I would never have allowed the method to work on myself. Had he somehow sensed my new vulnerability? Had I given myself away?

Mrs. Simmonds arranged the tea things for me to pour out and Brent and I watched her with silent absorption, as if she were about to perform a conjuring trick.

"Antique silver teapot—Meissen cups—and—and—sugar tongs!" He clapped his hands and gave a yowl of ecstasy. "Fantastic! Oh Miss Mitchell, this really is your scene."

It wasn't, I thought grimly; it was rapidly becoming his.

"Ah well." I made a sigh of world-weariness. "When somebody comes along with an unspecified request it is safest to give them the full works since as likely as not they are simply looking for journalistic copy."

That shut him up while Mrs. Simmonds finished with the tray, and she, at least, seemed to have recovered her poise, because I could see her smiling quietly to herself. But I wished I had been less ungracious, because it was going to be impossible to keep up this acid tone. Besides, he was a poor creature, puffed up beyond his capacities by the publicity machine, and now driven to use his cunning and his personal advantages to keep up with it. Not like Barry, who had had no such problem: only an iron determination to get to the top more quickly than anybody else and to stay there at all costs.

"I'm not going out till later," said Mrs. Simmonds, "but there's a radio programme I want to listen to, so if you'll excuse me—"

We nodded and smiled at each other and she left the room.

"Mr. Ashwood," I began.

"Brent," he interrupted, but I took no notice and went on:

"Before we get down to your business, do satisfy my curiosity and tell me what you and Mrs. Simmonds were laughing about when you came upstairs just now."

He went very red. "Oh. Did you hear?"

I watched his mind working as he tried to invent an innocuous joke.

"Never mind." I broke into his stutterings. "I can always ask her later if my curiosity has not abated. We usually have a little heart-to-heart chat in the evening, Mrs. Simmonds and I. It gets very lonely, you know, being vintage Helen Mitchell as you call it."

I gasped when I had spoken. I must indeed be going out of my mind, to break out into maudlin self-pity like this. Brent looked a bit embarrassed and I hoped he would quickly change the subject. People like to read and write sour-grapes sob stories about the loneliness and unhappiness of fame, but they don't actually want to come close enough to get a whiff of it, any more than they want to know what wrecked and wretched lives the big winners of football pools sometimes lead. It destroys their vision of the earthly paradise and, unless they have the good fortune to believe in a heavenly one, leaves them with nothing to dream of.

There was an uncomfortable moment while Brent fidgeted and spilt tea in his saucer and crumbs on the carpet and looked around the room again and especially at the roll-top desk.

Suddenly I began to laugh and had difficulty in stopping.

"It's too absurd," I said at last. "Just too banal to be true.

I'd never dare put a scene like this into a book and neither would you. Here am I—having got there and unlikely to be toppled, until after my death when the first boom is over and it becomes fashionable to wonder what anyone ever saw in me, and here you are, thinking you had got there and finding that you hadn't—for I assume that is your trouble?—and I start off by trying to show you that it isn't worth it. Oh no. It won't do. We really must do better than this."

I blew my nose, drank some tea, and tried to compose myself. The tendency to giggle was still strong in me. It was reinforced the next moment, because without any warning he suddenly slithered from his chair on to his knees, made an extraordinary leap and landed on his knees again by the side of my chair, folded his arms along the arm, laid his head upon them, and began to cry.

I drank some more tea and waited. His weeping continued and after a moment or two it didn't seem funny at all. The rush of memory, momentarily halted, hit me with renewed force. Barry had once collapsed into helpless sobbing like this, not long after we got to know each other, and when my shyness and uncertainty had led me to be rather cool to him, and it was that outbreak that changed the whole course of my life.

Brent shifted a little, raised his head so that his voice could be heard, and said:

"Oh God, I wish I was dead."

The very same words and the very same tone—unhappy, but reproachful too, as if it were somehow all my fault. I tried to recall my own response on that earlier occasion but without success. The days, months, years that followed were clear enough, but of what I myself had felt and said and done at the vital moment there was no trace. Perhaps, as now, I had felt nothing but embarrassment and a longing for the scene to be over; perhaps even then I had been incapable of any spontaneous outbursts of feeling, of any show of emotion that had not been filtered through the censor of my mind. Perhaps even then I had been creating fiction: mentally describing the scene as it took place and not living through it at all.

Perhaps I had never really loved Barry at all.

Then why had I thrown aside my own career and all my

own prospects in order to further his, and nearly died when we parted? And treasured every cautious letter he ever wrote to me, and every photograph and newspaper cutting, and put them in a large envelope which still lay in the top drawer of the roll-top desk because in fifteen years I had been unable either to look at its contents or to throw it away unopened. And my diaries—in small soft-covered notebooks—an intermittent record of the years with Barry, full of the wildest passionate outpourings, all that could not be written, could not be spoken, either to Barry or to anyone else.

But what had happened to this self-annihilating love when it lost its object? Did it disperse, leaving a vacuum? Or turn into hatred? Or transfer to somebody else? Or had it lain dormant, a seemingly extinct volcano, waiting to erupt again when least expected?

The questions worried me. I really wanted to understand. But there was nobody to ask. And I had to act Helen Mitchell and try to give some good advice to this boy who looked so like Barry.

Brent scrambled to his feet, muttered an angry apology, and then turned to the desk and pulled the rolling lid up and down several times.

I reached for a piece of cake and leaned back in my chair, feeling the sort of relief one feels when a screaming child or a big boisterous dog is removed from one's presence. Probably it had been like this on that earlier occasion—that I had said and done nothing at all; or perhaps I had been rigid with anxiety lest we might be interrupted, because it had been in an election committee-room, where people didn't trouble to knock before coming in.

"How tidy you keep your desk," exclaimed Brent. "Don't you ever get in a muddle—not even when inspiration is coming in full flood?"

"It's no hardship to me to be tidy," I said. "I'm rather obsessional about it."

He pulled the rolling lid down again and turned the key. Then he returned to sit on the edge of his chair and leaned forward, clasping his hands together and speaking earnestly:

"Miss Mitchell—where do you get your inspiration? How do you do it? That's what I wanted to see you about."

"You've run dry?"

"Absolutely. After one book!"

"Haven't you written anything since *Road Without End*?"
He blushed. "Unspeakable stuff. I tear it up at once for
fear I should happen to re-read it."

"Did you write anything before *Road Without End*?"

"Lots—but it's unspeakable too."

I was silent, wondering what on earth to suggest.

"I don't mind confessing to *you* that I'm stuck," went on
Brent, "but I wouldn't dare say it to anyone else. I pretend
that I'm working on something, but that I'm so busy being
celebrated that I haven't time to get on with it. But in fact
there's nothing—*nothing*!" He banged his fist on the arm of
the chair. "And I can't last out any longer."

"Have you any money left?" I asked.

"No."

"Then how—?"

"I get some social security. And there's Jean."

"Jean? Oh yes. The waitress. The dedication of *Road
Without End*. You imagined telling her this story—the story
of your life. She's still living with you? You live on her
wages?"

For a third time he went scarlet. "Put like that it sounds—
it sounds—"

"Oh, don't be silly, boy!" I cried. "I'm not making any
moral judgments. I'm only trying to get the facts straight
before making any suggestions. She's keeping you because
she loves you and believes she is your inspiration. But she
isn't any more. Only you haven't the heart or the nerve to tell
her so, and you are pretending to her that you are writing
another masterpiece. So she too is getting as impatient as
your agents and publishers and everybody else. Am I right?"

"Yes."

"You're in a mess, Brent Ashwood. Do you—or does
Jean—pay out any money to your two ex-wives, by the way?"

"No, thank God. Brenda's got a good job and in any case
they allowed her nothing because of her own adultery, and
Molly married a guy with a chain of do-it-yourself stores
who's got pots of money and was willing to take on the kid
too, provided I gave up all claim to it."

"You've been lucky. Shall you marry Jean?"

"I'd rather not. For a variety of reasons. Not all selfish."

"It does seem rather a good idea to call a halt. At this rate you'll have six divorces by the time you're forty. Charles Chaplin and Woolworth heiresses can do that sort of thing but it's outside your scope. How about taking a job—the more menial the better—and letting it be known that you are trying to recover the springs of creativity that have been cut off by the artificiality of the personality cult business? You ought to get a book out of that—how you were spoilt by success, all the disillusion and sterility, and how you went back to real life—oh, you know the sort of thing. You don't need me to tell you. It's a common form of second novel after the successful autobiographical first."

"I've tried it," he replied. "I got a job in a cardboard box factory about eight months ago. It was absolute hell and it didn't work at all."

"Oh dear." I pondered this and decided that he had probably told all his workmates that he was Brent Ashwood trying to find his soul and that they had expressed their opinion in similarly unrestrained terms. I tried to think of some other practical suggestions.

"Journalism?" I said. "Sports reporting? Film or TV writing? There must have been a few concrete offers in all the publicity over *Road Without End*."

This time his reply was more evasive and I guessed that he had managed to muff up all his chances, either through inexperience, or over-confidence, or over-exposure, or just plain getting people's backs up. He really was a most tiresome young man, with just enough rudimentary positive qualities to make them "credible"—in the hideous contemporary phrase. He had some genuine talent, and he had an occasional flicker of something that might be called conscience, and there was a sort of fundamental honesty, but that too was consciously employed to the best possible effect.

An exploiter. That was what he was. Not exactly a parasite, because he did have a genuine contribution to make, which a parasite has not, but he had studied the art of exploitation and made himself adept at it. Just as Barry had done, and like Barry he had no lack of willing victims. But he would never get to the top; he was too petty; he hadn't Barry's ruthlessness. Suddenly I felt a keen sense of disappointment that he was not like Barry in this respect.

"What were you doing before the book?" I asked, hurrying on with the questions in order to suppress my own train of thought. "Any hope of picking up any threads there?"

"None at all. It was nothing—all geared towards writing the book."

We seemed to have come to an end. He had thought out all the more obvious solutions to his problem for himself and I had nothing more to suggest. What did he want of me? Could he possibly be hoping that I was going to offer to help him write a book? The idea was not so very fantastic, though Brent could not possibly know that. I had, after all, written all Barry's speeches for him, even before I gave up the deputy headship of a school in order to become his political agent; I had written his letters, election addresses, even pamphlets that went out under his name. At the time I had believed that he really did have difficulty in drafting such documents himself, although the ideas were never lacking. Only years later, but still well before our final break, did I realize that he could perfectly well have done it himself but preferred to spend the time on more lucrative activities—correcting exam papers, cramming wealthy private pupils, and so on. And if he could get a fool of a woman to handle his image-creation free, or on the pittance meted out by the party, well, why not? His own wife was useless in this respect—a frightened little girl who had been a children's nurse. Or so I believed at the time. Only later did I realize that she had done her full share of image-creating too. With brilliant juggling skill Barry had played us off one against the other, as later he was to play off his political opponents. He never even bothered to waste much time on it. He had a fine instinct for calculating exactly what each one of us would put up with, how far he could go before the worm showed signs of turning. If he thought I was becoming restive he would tackle it at once, with some automatic endearments, a few hints of the frustrations of his home life, and a supremely simple blackmail line: "I can't do without you."

He was like a drug that paralysed the muscles and the will. The mind revolted but had no ability to act.

I sighed heavily, dragging myself back into the present. This good-looking weakling sitting opposite to me now had none of Barry's hypnotic power. I could get rid of him any moment if I really wanted to. The weakness lay in myself. But so it had lain before; there had been others against whom all Barry's technique had been employed in vain.

"I'm very sorry, Brent," I said, "but I can't think of anything else."

The desperate look returned to his eyes; he seemed to be able to summon it up at will, just as Barry had done. For a moment it seemed as if he was going to fall at my feet again but he just sat there, balanced rather uneasily on the arm of the chair, staring at the roll-top desk as if it held the object of all his desires.

As indeed, in a sense, it did.

"Unless," I began slowly and then stopped.

An extraordinary notion had come into my mind. My books meant nothing to me, my money and my beautiful home were worthless without the human relationships that put the kick of life into inanimate things. I would bargain the lot for just another taste of the complete abandonment of my early years with Barry. Now I know that I am going mad, I said to myself; but the notion would not be put aside.

Brent jumped up and came towards me, the desperate look gone, the face hopeful and sunny and appealing.

"You've had an idea!" he cried.

I thought rapidly. It must be subtly hinted at, a little temptation held out in such a way that he would believe the plot to be his own. I could hardly cry aloud: Be my lover, give me back some reason for living, and all the glory and praise that accrue from putting dead words on paper shall be yours.

"What you need," I said firmly, "is something that catches your imagination at this very moment—something *new*. All the themes I've suggested have gone stale on you. They would be re-hashing old stuff and you haven't the experience yet to make a success of them. Why don't you start off with just our present situation—young man in search of a story approaches successful lady novelist—and see where it takes you?"

"Good lord," he cried, "I believe that might work!"

"You need a woman to inspire you, obviously. Well, here I am. See what you can do along those lines and stop getting yourself married and divorced for a while."

He was moving about excitedly, jerking his head so that the thick fair main swung from side to side. A handsome

young animal; it gave me great pleasure to watch him—the
sort of pleasure I had thought never to experience again.

Then he came to a standstill and frowned. "I can see the
story beginning, but how do I go on with it?"

"Good heavens," I cried, "have I got to give you the whole
novel? You'll have to work it out for yourself."

"If you could just give me a line—some idea of how the
plot might develop—"

"My dear boy! Give me a chance. I'll have to brood over
it myself. Even I can't produce a plan for an entire novel in
five minutes."

This was a lie. I could see in a flash how the plot could
develop, what my own future could be. The short burst of an
Indian summer, and then the long, slow, painful and shameful descent into the darkness. Jealousies, recrimination, humiliation, the grasping at straws. The complete disintegration
of a character—just as it took place in my books. Was it really
going to happen to me? Had my fictional imagination been
able to see into the future? Nonsense, I told myself firmly: I
plan my books, I plan my life—it is not surprising that they
should resemble each other. I wanted some happiness and I
was fully prepared to pay for it. It was a hard-headed bargain.

"I think the best plan," I said aloud as if after weighty
consideration, "would be for me to think it over for the rest
of today and if you come along tomorrow afternoon I should
be in a position to develop the idea if you want me to."

And to frame it in such a way that you want to come again
and yet again, I added to myself.

He sat down opposite me to express his thanks at length.
Memories stirred once more and mingled with present sensations. I could have stretched out my hand and touched his
cheek, his hair. But not today; it was too early. I clasped my
hands together, but still I could sense under my fingers the
rough warm texture of his skin. My voice was very cool:

"It will be something of an experiment—the transplanting
of ideas."

"Let's hope it takes."

At the door of the room he paused; I had got up too and
was standing a foot or two away from him.

"But Miss Mitchell," he said, awkward again, "what
about your own work? I mean, shouldn't you be working on

a novel now? And if you're going to waste your time thinking
up a plot for me—"

"Oh that's all right," I replied airily. "I've plots enough
to spare. I'm really quite excited about this—it makes a nice
change. Besides, there's no need for me to write anything for
a long time yet. I've got a couple of typescripts ready for
press whenever they are needed."

I had not meant to say this, it slipped out before I could
stop it, and I was horrified to find that my words were so
little under my control.

Brent's eyes opened very wide and yet again he looked at
the roll-top desk.

"You've written two more books? You keep them here, at
home? Is that wise?"

I tried to make light of it. "You think they might be stolen?
They wouldn't be much use to anyone else, you know. They
are typical Helen Mitchells and, as is constantly being pointed
out, I have a rather distinctive style."

"All the same," he began. He was pink and embarrassed
but it still gave me pleasure to look at him, a rather savage
pleasure now. "Wouldn't it be better to keep them at the bank
or somewhere?" he went on.

"I'll think about it. And I'll think about your story. And
you go home and put down some impressions straight away—
now, while vintage Helen Mitchell is fresh in your mind. Run
along now."

I badly wanted him to go. I needed to be alone to digest
all these new feelings that had come over me, this uprush of
sheer physical sensation that was threatening to overwhelm
me completely and cause me to lose all control.

"I don't know how to thank you," he stammered.

"Then don't try."

It was all I could say. I was holding the door open, my
right hand gripping the smooth brass knob, my left hand
hanging at my side, heavy, aching to find its way on to that
thick fair hair. Suddenly it seemed to be moving upwards of
its own accord. I started and nearly lost my balance. Then I
realized that he had taken my hand and was carrying it to his
lips. A florid, reverential gesture, only to be attempted by a
young man who could alternate so rapidly between awkwardness and self-assurance and look equally appealing in both.

So my mind described the little scene, but my mind was no longer the dominant part of me. It worked half-heartedly, taking refuge in conventional phrases, while all the time my heart was racing and my limbs were without strength. For a long time after he had gone I sat on the sofa staring at the back of my hand and every now and then raising it to my lips as if their own touch could revive the sensation that his had aroused in that spot.

4

How long I sat in this sensuous reverie I did not know. The mental treadmill gave a few half-hearted turns and then all was still. The miracle has happened, I said over and over again when all the other phrases had slipped from my mind; I am alive once more.

There was a knock at the door and the plump form of Mrs. Simmonds, clothed in pink crimplene, appeared.

"Oh," she said. "He's gone. I didn't hear him leave."

"I expect you had the radio on loud," I replied. It was an enormous effort to make this little remark; my whole consciousness was concentrated on the sensation of Brent's kissing my hand.

"How did it go?" asked Mrs. Simmonds, after waiting in vain for me to speak.

"Oh, all right."

I wished she would hurry up and go away; I wanted to linger in my dream, but I was not so far gone in my lunacy that I did not realize the necessity for appearing as usual.

"He's a very bumptious young man," she said. "Do you know, Miss Mitchell, he actually had the cheek to ask me, when I was showing him up, what was the best way of softening you up!"

"Did he indeed?" All of a sudden I was intensely interested. I had momentarily forgotten, in the excitement of what had happened to me since, my previous curiosity about the little conversation on the stairs. There was a faint stab of jealousy, but it was outweighed by the pleasure of talking about Brent.

"What exactly did he say?" I asked, trying hard to speak with the cool detachment that Mrs. Simmonds would expect of me, though in fact I was as tremblingly eager as a young girl awaiting a message from a lover too shy to declare himself in person.

Mrs. Simmonds gave me a sharp glance, but answered as if my pretence had been successful.

"That was all—just what I said. That he was frightened of you but determined to ask you for help. And that living here as I did, I must know you very well, and what would be the best way to get round you. The cheek of it!"

"Oh well, he's that sort of person," I said. "There are a lot of them like that nowadays, I'm afraid."

We spent a few moments silently registering indignation while Mrs. Simmonds finished the clearing away and I debated how to prolong the conversation without arousing suspicion.

"But what was the joke?" I asked at last. "There was great laughter just before you came in. Did you tell him how to 'soften me up'?"

I was glad I thought of saying this; it had the true ring of the Helen Mitchell she knew; it would throw her off the scent.

She began to bluster. "You know I never talk about you."

"But you must have said something—or he must have—to make you laugh."

Suddenly she became very stiff. "I believe he was trying to—to chat me up, as they say. I suppose he thought it would help him in his application to you. He said something rather insolent which I would prefer not to repeat, if you don't mind. I expect you can guess the sort of thing. I only hope you were not subjected to the same sort of treatment."

"Oh no," I cried gaily. "He didn't try to get fresh with me."

It was all I could do not to laugh. Here we were, two worthy ladies past our first youth, getting ourselves into a great state of excitement over a beautiful young man. I could see the situation in all its absurdity and yet I had no compulsion to transform it into a mental drama. Neither did it have the least effect on my own feelings about Brent; my determination to bind him to me, with every weapon that I had at my command, was as strong as ever. But it would be as well to start preparing Mrs. Simmonds for the frequent visits that Brent would be making to the house.

"I have made rather a foolish promise, though," I added ruefully.

She relaxed a little and looked interested; there was no longer any pretence of being busy with the tea-things.

"As I thought," I continued, "it was this problem of being unable to write another book that was troubling him. He must have guessed that I would be an easy prey for someone in such trouble, and of course I said I would help him."

"But you can't write a book for him," said Mrs. Simmonds. We were slipping back into our former roles: I was calmly authoritative, she was deferential in a self-contained manner.

"I can't indeed, although that might be simpler than what I am going to try to do, which is to imbue him with the ideas to write his own. It may not be possible. We shall have to see."

I got up and moved to my desk—a gesture of dismissal.

"Oh, by the way," I said, turning around just as Mrs. Simmonds was leaving the room, "he'll be coming again tomorrow afternoon, but we won't trouble about the VIP treatment. If you would provide a few cakes we will get tea or coffee ourselves. It's really more in the nature of a working session."

"Very well," said Mrs. Simmonds.

I could tell that she was annoyed, but since she had no justification for being so, she could not allow herself the relief of showing it.

"And I'm going out for a walk now. It's a lovely evening. It's a pity to stay indoors. If anyone rings tell them I will call back."

"Very well," she said again.

I collected my handbag and a book in case. I decided to sit out and read, and I stepped into the evening sunshine. The business traffic had all dispersed and there were not many cars going by. People were strolling along the promenade in twos and threes and I no longer had any envy of them. I crossed the road and leaned against the railing at the spot where I had seen Brent do so. It was only a few hours ago and yet it seemed like an age. I had been confused and frightened then, uneasily straddling the gulf between past and present. And now I no longer cared. I felt as I had sometimes felt as a child when riding a bicycle down a steep hill. At first there is fear, a great horror of the imagination at what might happen if the machine should run out of control; and then comes the moment of release, when all fear is swallowed up in the ecstasy of rushing movement—a force far greater than oneself is whirling one along, there is no means of stopping, all one can do is cling to the handlebars and steer.

In those rides, however, I had known where I was going. In my present plunge I had no sight of the end. But what did it matter? I was growing old and I had had years enough of substitute life.

I began to walk along the promenade, towards the tower blocks and the pier, which straddled out, a thin dark line against the pale glittering sea. He shall take me out to dinner, I decided, to the theatre and to the opera at Glyndebourne. We will go for drives in the country, spend days in London, go for a holiday abroad.

It was at this point in my plans that I suddenly realized that I had walked the whole way from the terrace to the pier without the least hint of the panic of agoraphobia, so utterly absorbed had I been in my dreams. When I saw how far I was from home there was a faint return of the anxiety, but it was more from habit than anything else and only lasted a moment. I walked on, put down a coin and pushed through the turnstile on to the pier. I strolled along the sunny side, my eye remarking the red faces, shut eyes and open mouths of the few people still sprawling in canvas chairs, but my mind made no attempt to capture them in words. It was enough just to exist and to dream of Brent.

Between the terrace and the main road was a little strip of garden, consisting of rough grass and a few wind-battered shrubs, and on my return I sat down on the wooden bench, revelling in the fresh air and new-found freedom, and reluctant to go in. A tall thin man with a bald head and rimless spectacles came up and greeted me—my next-door neighbour, a retired accountant who had lived all alone in the big house since the death of his wife the previous year.

"Good evening, Mr. Thorburn," I beamed at him. "Isn't it a lovely evening? I've just been for a walk."

"Then I'm too late to ask if you will join me in mine," he said.

"I'm afraid so. Enjoy yourself."

He ought to have moved on then, but rather to my annoyance he perched himself on the arm of the bench. It reminded me of Mrs. Simmonds. A sort of half-way-house gesture, indicating a desire to stay and chat and at the same time an anxiety not to appear to intrude. A common phenomenon of modern social life; I must tell Brent about it. I couldn't help smiling at the thought of expressing such thoughts as these to Brent.

"You're looking very well, Miss Mitchell, if I may take the liberty of saying so," said Mr. Thorburn. "It's good to see you taking a rest from your labours of providing us all with the delights of mystery and suspense."

"Thank you," I murmured, trying not to laugh. Silly old man. What a bore he was.

"I don't write all the time, you know," I went on. "In fact I've decided to give myself a long rest from it."

"You are going to take a holiday? Will you be going abroad?"

"Possibly. I don't know yet."

But I did know. I was going to take a holiday with Brent and the thought made me smile with pleasure. Mr. Thorburn took it for an invitation to sit down on the bench and tell me that his wife had always wanted to go to Greece but somehow they had never got round to it and now it was too late. I looked interested and let my mind wander. I was reclining in a long chair under Mediterranean skies, my hand was trailing on the sand and every now and then I would throw a few grains of sand on to Brent's mahogany tanned back.

It appeared that Mr. Thorburn had asked a question and was waiting for a reply.

"Yes, yes," I murmured vaguely.

After a little misunderstanding it turned out that I had accepted an invitation to lunch. It was all I could do not to giggle. The first result of my falling in love with Brent had been to acquire me an elderly admirer.

The second result was less innocent and amusing. It consisted of a quarrel between myself and Marian Gray, my friend since early childhood. Marian was one of the very few people who knew the full story of my long love affair with another woman's husband, all except for the one incident which I could not tell her or anybody else. That one incident, which was the cause of my final break with Barry, had been confided to my diary alone. The story of it—from my point of view of course—was contained in one of the notebooks that had remained untouched for years in the top drawer of the roll-top desk.

Marian and I had little in common except memories. She had a small private income, and by living modestly and doing a certain amount of private coaching, she had been able to retire early from full-time teaching and to devote the greater part of her time to an almost maniacal pursuit of her hobby of photography, which didn't interest me at all. She was a biochemist, disliked literary people, and had barely read half a dozen novels in her life. Perhaps it was for this very reason that we retained each other's goodwill and that it was never marred by envy.

At least that was how I looked at it until the Wednesday following Brent's first visit.

Brent and I had progressed a long way since then. I managed to control my first raptures to such an extent that he began the second visit with almost the same degree of awkwardness as he had shown on the first. I was very matter-of-fact, concentrating exclusively on the novel that he was to write. There would be plenty of time later to talk to him as I wanted to talk. The pleasure of saving up my thoughts and feelings to relate to Brent was not lessened by postponement. He was my form of reference, the audience ever present in my heart and mind. In due course he would hear it all, but first I must make sure of him.

He had written a chapter of a book and he produced it somewhat shamefacedly. I sent him out to the kitchen to make tea while I read. It might have been worse, but the picture of the lady novelist was very much the public image of myself.

"You'll have to conquer your inhibitions if you're going to breathe life into it," I said, after a few words of commendation.

"But it's so awkward—I mean if I'm to use you as a

model—I mean I might want to write something not quite
flattering—''

He stammered his way to silence. I raised my eyebrows.

''I doubt if anything you could say about any character
based on myself could shock, surprise, or hurt me. I have no
illusions whatever either about myself or anybody else. However, I see your point and I certainly won't ask you to let me
see all you write. All I ask is that you should keep in touch
because, my dear Brent, I am thinking of trying the experiment of writing a novel on the same theme, using the same
jumping-off point. It will be interesting to compare the two
versions in due course.''

He protested, looking very handsome and lively as he did
so.

''Now that's not fair, Helen Mitchell! I can't compete with
you. I can't have one of my miserable little efforts put alongside another of your triumphs. It isn't fair, is it?''

He sat down opposite me in his favorite position, leaning
forwards with his hands clasped between his knees. His expression was impudent, wheedling. I found it very difficult
to control my hands and my voice.

''Even supposing that we both finish our novels,'' I said,
''it is extremely unlikely that anyone will ever notice that they
set out from the same starting-point. Have you ever seen the
work of a group of art students in a life class? It varies so
much that one can hardly believe they are drawing from the
same model. Or schoolchildren's essays on a given topic. I
used to be a teacher, you know. It's rather fun to try my skill
again, though I never dreamed of anything so ambitious as
teaching somebody to write a novel.''

''I don't know why you're taking all this trouble over me,''
he said.

''You'll find out,'' I replied airily.

In this way I succeeded in holding his interest. If there
seemed to be the least danger of its flagging I had only to
make some remark about my unpublished manuscripts. He
was still fascinated by the desk and could not keep his eyes
off it.

So several afternoons went by. Mrs. Simmonds kept out
of the way, and on the occasions when we were obliged to
speak to each other we were both very cool and formal. She

prepared an evening meal for Marian and myself as usual and
then departed for her evening of bingo with a friend.

"I don't think she likes me being here," said Brent, who
had lingered on longer than I wanted him to, for Marian was
due any moment and I didn't want her to meet him yet. I was
not yet hardened enough to carry out my act with him in
front of a critical observer.

"I hope I can invite whom I like to my house without
asking permission from my housekeeper," I said haughtily.

He held up his hands to his head and mimed the action of
dodging a missile. Then we both laughed and I looked pointedly at my watch.

"Can't I stay and see you in action with your friend?" he
asked. "I might want to write a scene about it."

"All right then. Just for a few minutes."

In spite of the awkwardness of the situation I could not
help but be pleased that he wanted to stay.

Marian greeted him in her abrupt, rather offhand way. His
name obviously meant nothing to her. He slipped on the
charm but instantly let it go again as he realized that it would
have no effect on her, and he stood there looking a little
foolish, as if he had mislaid his clothes and didn't know how
to behave without them. I was intensely conscious of every
movement he made, of every fleeting change of expression
on his face. I knew his thoughts; I knew what he was going
to say and do.

"Same time tomorrow?"

He turned to me, eyes and mouth working again, pointedly
excluding Marian and at the same time showing her that here
was a woman who did respond to him.

"Yes, please," I said. "There's a little job I'd like to ask
you to do for me. I'll explain about it when you come."

"Another mystery! I just can't wait to find out. 'Bye for
now, Helen."

It was the first time he had called me that. Done deliberately, I thought, and with bravado because of Marian's presence. I was delighted but at the same time embarrassed and
a little anxious. I did not want to arouse Marian's suspicions
and to face her protests; I would have to try to put her off the
scent.

Suddenly I had an inspiration—the sort of inspiration that

would sometimes come during the writing of a novel, to help
one over a little difficulty in the plot. I could kill two birds
with one stone. In a single stroke I could both bind Brent to
me and provide an excellent reason for his presence. The
moment he had left the room I burst out without giving Marian a chance to speak:

"I'm going to try him out as my new secretary. Mrs. Fairbrother's baby is due in six weeks and she doesn't want to
work for much longer."

Marian was disconcerted.

"I thought you said he was a writer."

" 'Was' is the operative word. He's run dry after one book,
is out of a job, and badly in need of both moral support and
cash. And I want someone to handle the alterations I'm having done to the house—converting the basement flat, in particular—and to drive me about and be generally useful. You
know I loathe hired cars and public transport. Besides, the
idea appeals to me. Eminent lady novelist and glamorous
young male secretary. Think of the tongue-wagging it will
cause. And how much it will annoy Philip and Dora."

Philip was my only surviving brother, a respectable solicitor in the City of London. He was born worried and some
of my earliest memories were of my attempts to scandalize
him.

Marian looked only partially reassured.

"I shouldn't have thought you needed to seek for any more
publicity," she said. "However, it's your business."

We served up our meal and exchanged our week's news. It
was all very much as usual, except that there was just the
faintest air of constraint, the cloud no bigger than a man's
hand. If there was a television programme that appealed to
us both, I thought, we might manage to get through the evening without further reference to Brent. I flicked through the
Radio Times while we were drinking our coffee; the relevant
pages were barren of interest.

"What ghastly photographs of people they do rake up for
this paper," I said as I flung the *Radio Times* aside. "D'you
think they use passport photographs?"

It was a rhetorical question but it gave her an opening to
launch forth on to her hobby, had she so chosen. But of course

she saw through my crude attempt to divert her thoughts. We knew each other too well for it to succeed.

"Possibly," she said indifferently, and we were silent for a few minutes.

Oh well, I said to myself with resignation, it has to come sooner or later; let's get it over now.

"I don't like your gigolo type, Nell," she said presently, sitting foursquare on the sofa and stirring her coffee with unnecessary energy.

I wasn't offended; we could say this sort of thing to each other.

"No, I didn't think you would," I replied. "He does rather labour at it. But he's quite agreeable in spite of it."

"He reminds me of Barry Walters," she said.

This gave me a shock. It was many years since Barry's name had been mentioned between us. Marian had borne my ecstasies and my torments with great loyalty and fortitude, putting up with cancelled engagements, late arrivals, spoiled meals, wasted theatre tickets—all the symptoms of neglect and discourtesy that resulted from my putting Barry's least little wish above every other call on my time and attention. All my friends had disliked Barry and most of them had drifted away, giving me up as a hopeless case. Marian alone stuck on, detached, critical, but always available.

"Someone has to hang around to pick up the pieces," she would say when, in fits of misery and self-disgust, I would tell her to leave me alone. Only once did she very nearly take me at my word and that was when I refused to marry a cousin of hers, also a biochemist. He was a paragon of a man—kind, intelligent, witty, reliable, and personally not unattractive. I liked him enormously; I had absolutely nothing whatever against him except for the fact that he was not Barry.

Somehow or other Marian managed to forgive me, but her dislike of Barry deepened into a hatred that was, I think, the strongest emotion of her life. I don't know what she would have done if she had known the very worst about him. Fortunately she had never had the least suspicion of the true cause of the final breach.

"Does he?" I said with assumed indifference. "Do you know, I've practically forgotten what Barry looked like."

"You see him on television often enough," she said almost brutally.

"I never watch the news or current affairs programmes."

She glared at me and then got up and stumped over to my desk, where the morning's *Times* was lying. I had scarcely glanced at it; my whole morning had been filled with dreams of Brent.

"There you are," she said, handing me the folded paper.

The photograph of Barry was on the front page. He was shaking hands with some eminent American environmentalist. Lord Walters—Britain's great champion of the quality of life, tireless campaigner against pollution, the most influential man in the government, it was said, feared by all Ministers, scourge of selfish commercial interests, St. George in shining armour, a model of integrity and selfless devotion on eight thousand a year . . .

I wanted to laugh, I wanted to cry. Marian was looking at me with a sort of angry triumph. But she hasn't the least idea of what I am thinking, I said to myself. Did she really believe that the blurred press photograph of this highly esteemed gentleman, suave, smirking, flabby and overweight, was going to kindle the embers of a long dead passion? What was her intention? To prove to me that he hadn't been worth it? As if I didn't know!

"Oh," I said, "I didn't notice it. He hasn't worn well, has he?"

She gave a snort.

"He hasn't changed all that much. Don't you notice the likeness?"

I studied the photograph more closely. It was the first time for many years that I had brought myself to linger over a picture of Barry in all his glory; during all this time I had quickly turned the page or switched off the television set when his image appeared. I was conscious of a curious sensation that I could not quite place; it seemed to contain almost as much pity as pain. Pity for Barry? Absurd. If ever a man had no need of pity, he was that one.

I made a grimace, shrugged my shoulders, and handed the paper back to Marian, hoping she would say no more. I didn't want to talk about Brent, and it would be ridiculous to quarrel about Barry now, after all these years of self-control.

"And neither have you changed, Nell," went on Marian. "After all you've achieved and all the reputation you've won for yourself, you're as feeble as ever where men are concerned. You fall hook, line and sinker for a bit of cheap flattery and you still have to go and pick yourself a rotter. You—in your position! It's disgusting."

She had never before spoken so enthusiastically of my work. I was touched, and at the same time grieved that her praise should come to light in this particular context. But I was not going to apologize for Brent. I could not give him up now, not even for Marian. Besides, it was no longer about him that we were arguing. This was a time-bomb, planted many years ago. Our minds were in the past.

"I didn't pick Barry," I said mildly, "he picked me."

"You were ripe for the plucking."

This was said with more than Marian's normal bluntness. There was resentment, almost spite, in it. I looked at her with surprise and it suddenly flashed through my mind that, so far from hating Barry, Marian had herself been in love with him—deeply and painfully in love, with all the self-loathing and frustration, all the passionate hopelessness that must accompany the love of a plain and unattractive woman for a man who does not even think of her as a woman at all. So that was why she had stuck to me—to live through my feelings, to get some queer twisted satisfaction out of my own passion, not quite so frustrated, for Barry. How self-centred I had been! How incredibly blind one could be about people whom one knew very well. I ought to have been exceptionally perceptive, with my novelist's insight and imagination, and yet I had managed to remain in ignorance of this simple fact for all these years. I wished I had not glimpsed the truth now. It was as disconcerting and disagreeable as if I had been an unwilling eavesdropper at a confessional.

"Oh well, it's all old history," I said.

"And to think that you might have married Geoffrey," she persisted, "and saved him from tying himself up to that dreadful neurotic woman."

"Now look here, Marian," I said, stung into sharpness, "I will not be held responsible for other people's marital errors. We all have to look out for ourselves in this life."

"Such a waste," she said, "such a stupid waste of a life."

"To whose life are you referring? Yours or mine?"

I said this sarcastically; it was not surprising that she glared at me again. I was very unhappy and yet I could not help thinking that it would be very convenient to break off relations with Marian, because it would mean I should no longer have to worry about her criticisms of Brent.

She got to her feet. "Of course if you want to go making a fool of yourself all over again at your age," she began.

"Of course if you get jealous just because I've found myself a good-looking young secretary," I mimicked.

"I'd better go." She picked up her bag. "Not much point our talking any more tonight, is there, Nell? I'll give you a ring."

"Yes, you do that."

The moment she had left the house I began to tell Brent all about it in my mind. She's rather a bore, I would say; poor thing—I don't suppose she's ever got beyond the chastest of kisses in her life—Lesbian or otherwise.

Even in this imaginary conversation I was already putting Marian into the past. Probably we should speak to each other again occasionally but the regular weekly visit would have to come to an end.

And thus my mind lightly disposed of one of the two remaining people who held the various strands of my life together.

5

Brent was delighted when I suggested he should act as my secretary.

"You won't think it beneath your dignity, will you," I said, "to type my letters and make phone calls and attend to all the tiresome chores in the basement flat? I want it modernized and occupied but can't face the prospect of chivvying up builders and plumbers and all the rest."

"May I see it?" he asked.

We spent a very happy hour pottering around the musty, empty rooms, planning the changes and discussing the decorations with great enthusiasm. Another inspiration had come to me, but I did not breathe a word of it to Brent. Better to spin out the handing out of goodies; keep him always hoping and expecting.

Besides, there was Mrs. Simmonds. It would be best to get rid of her before actually bringing Brent on to the premises, but on the other hand I really did need somebody to look after the house and I didn't want to upset her too much. I was not unduly worried about this, however. It was only another little hold-up in the plot and something would soon spring to mind.

When we returned upstairs Brent seated himself on the round-backed chair at the desk.

"Do I type here?" he asked.

"If you like, though Mrs. Fairbrother always preferred to sit at the table."

"I like it here. Perhaps it will inspire me."

He moved his hands over the blotter, the box of writing-paper, the pen-tray, and other objects on the desk, finally allowing them to slip to the handles of the long top drawer, which he tugged at gently. Of course it did not give.

I smiled to myself behind his back. That's too obvious, I said to myself; you're going to have to wait a bit and to do a good deal of work before you get your reward, and it may not be quite the reward you are thinking of, even then.

"Where do you keep the typing paper?" he asked, as if it was that for which he had been searching.

"Here in the bottom drawer."

"Oh, thanks."

We wrote some letters and made a few phone calls and then I announced that it was time for sherry break. We relaxed side by side on the settee.

"If your novel doesn't turn out well," I said, "you can always fall back on your recollections of the last years of Helen Mitchell, by one who was her intimate companion during this period. That will sell all right and put you on the map again. It always does. Like Somerset Maugham. Or that novel by Beverley Nichols based on the last years of Melba. The singer, you know," I added when I saw how blank he looked. "The great Australian soprano."

"Oh yes," he said hastily. It was obvious that he still did not know what I was talking about, but I was gratified to see how anxious he was to please me and to adjust himself to my conversation.

"But Helen," he went on after a moment's pause, "you're not going to die—at your age!"

"Perhaps not. Perhaps I am. Who knows? What are you plotting to do with me in your book?"

I twisted round and looked at him keenly. He went very red.

"I'd rather—I'd rather not say."

I burst out laughing. "You're killing me off, are you? That's all right, Brent. My own plot is going much the same way. I always have a murder or attempted murder, you know. People expect it of me. I have this character who suffers a mental breakdown and a complete personality change and who ends up either planning to kill somebody else or as the victim of one of the other characters. It's a foolproof formula. I've done it again and again. The main problem is that one runs out of methods of killing—methods that a respectable person would be able to use, I mean. Of course I don't deal in thugs or gangsters.''

I caught myself up suddenly. I was talking too much.

"Sorry, Brent," I said. "Here I go again, holding forth when I really only want to hear how you are getting on. Or would you rather I didn't ask?"

It was clear from his face that he had not the least suspicion of my own doubts and fears. He was thinking only of himself.

"I was writing like mad most of last night," he said, "but I'd rather not show you yet, if you don't mind. I know you understand that the character isn't really you but just a starting-off point to get me going, and you know I can't begin to thank you for all you're doing for me. But it's a bit embarrassing, with me working for you—I mean, with both of us being writers, we both realize how distinct from each other fiction and real life are, even though the one feeds on the other. I mean, I wouldn't want you for one moment to think—"

He broke off. You're getting cocky, I thought, classing us together as writers. I permitted myself to put a hand on his arm. It felt hard and resilient through the fine blue cloth.

"My dear Brent," I said, "there is no need for you to explain or apologize. I fully understand your position. After all, I have placed you in it, and I take full responsibility for any circumstances that might arise in our real lives as a result of this experiment in the art of creative writing that I have devised."

I withdrew my hand and smiled at him again.

"It's rather fun, isn't it? I was getting terribly bored with my own career, you know."

"Well it looks as if you'll be the saving of mine. I suppose it's all right—what I'm writing, I mean. But it's not the same as it was with *Road Without End*. I mean they were all terribly ordinary people—my mother and the others. They could have been anybody's relations. But with you . . .''

His voice trailed away and I continued to look at him. In some respects his face was at its most attractive during these self-deprecating moods of his. I tried not to hear the faint whining note in his voice.

"I know I'm a bit of a scrounger," he went on, "and I haven't any morals and I've no scruples about making use of people if they're fool enough to let me, but there are some things that even I wouldn't dream of doing."

"Yes, Brent dear, I know. I perfectly understand that there are some things that you would not do."

His eyes turned to the roll-top desk and then quickly moved away again.

"So long as we know where we stand," he said, draining his glass and standing up. "Oughtn't I be doing some more work?"

"You certainly ought. We'll get those conversion plans drawn up right away."

The next few weeks were delightful. Agoraphobia was a thing of the past. We spent hours going round showrooms, leafing through catalogues, listening to sales representatives. Like ninety-nine people out of a hundred, both male and female, Brent was convinced that he had a flair for interior decoration. Being myself the one per cent exception, I allowed him full say. His vanity was flattered and it really looked, at that stage of our relationship, as if he was enjoying himself as much as I was.

Local shops having exhausted their interest for us, it became necessary to make a trip to London.

"We'll hire a big estate car," I said. "Then we can get around and pick up some of the small things straight away."

Brent was a wild driver. When he saw that I wasn't in the least bit nervous he cast off all his attempts at caution and flung the big Volvo about with delighted abandon. What does it matter, I thought, if it all ends now. I had to come a crash before very long in any case; I was well launched on my crazy rush downhill with no brakes.

"You're rather a marvellous person, you know," said Brent when we stopped for a snack in a pub. "Every other woman I've known in my life would be screaming their heads off if I drove like that."

"They value their lives. I don't."

"But Helen, with so much to live for—you in your position—"

I burst out laughing.

"Fame doesn't bring happiness. There you are! There's a nice bit of dialogue for your novel. Terrible, isn't it? Are you going to use it?"

"Well, as a matter of fact it isn't going quite the way I thought it would. I'd rather not talk about it too much if you don't mind."

"My dear, of course not." I was very sympathetic again. "Much better not to. It only lets the steam escape, scatters to waste the concentrated imaginative essence."

I took a gulp of my lager and tried to conceal a little shivering fit that had come upon me. It was not a recurrence of agoraphobia, although in fact this was the sort of excursion that had for a long time been very difficult for me. It was less acute than the familiar panic and yet in a way it was even worse: a sort of waking dream. Not a nightmare; a delightful dream. But was it real? Was I really sitting here in this mock Tudor saloon bar, with the plates of sandwiches on the round oak table in front of me and the rambler roses brushing against the leaded windows? Would I find myself, any moment now, seated at my desk, large pad of ruled foolscap before me, blue ballpoint pen in hand, rapidly covering pages with sprawling writing, now sighing, now smiling as the moods of my characters swung from sadness to joy, my whole being suffused with their beings, my mind and hand a mere vessel for the outpourings of their emotions?

A crisis of identity. The words came to me from somewhere. Perhaps my companion had uttered them. A phrase much beloved of reviewers, but I had never really understood what it meant. Attacking the phrase in my mind, I began to recover my balance. Always, in moments of panic, the critical faculty was my lifeline. I must have said something aloud, because I heard Brent reply.

I took another drink and looked around me.

"Do you know, I believe this is where Barry and I came on one of the few occasions when we were on an outing of pleasure. Although even that was mixed with business. We were on the way to a party conference in Brighton."

"Oh. Was he a politician?" asked Brent, with apparent interest. I had spoken to him of Barry but had not mentioned his present elevated position.

"Yes," I replied. "I acted as his election agent. He held one of the West Country constituencies—a safe seat, of course. I was a sort of PRO—an image creator. I was quite good at it. Being in love helped, of course. And the campaigning was convenient, since his wife remained at home in London with the children. They had three little girls who all made very undistinguished marriages and were heard of no more. His wife's death did merit a tiny paragraph in most of the national dailies, however."

"He was quite successful, then, was he?" asked Brent, with greater interest than before.

"Yes. He did very well."

Belated caution stopped me from saying more. I had intended to indulge myself by reminiscing to Brent but I did not want to let him know Barry's identity and I hoped that I had not gone too far to draw back. It was so difficult to know where to stop. Talking about the past helped to relieve this frightening feeling of unreality, this sensation of living in one of my books, not in my own life. The memories were more solid than the present moment.

"We stopped here on the way," I repeated, "and we stayed at the Albion. Of course we had to be very discreet for the sake of Barry's reputation and I used to hate that. There were times when I would have given all I had and all he had, just for the pleasure of calling him 'Darling' in public. And yet the people legitimately exercising that privilege probably loathed each other and barely spoke to each other in private. Oh well. That was twenty years ago. Things have changed a lot since. Adultery no longer casts a shadow over a man's public life. What does cast such a shadow? What's the dirty word today?"

I was thinking aloud, talking myself back into a firm hold on the present moment, in which existed my passion for Brent. My questions were rhetorical and I was startled when he replied firmly:

"Pollution. That's the unforgivable sin nowadays. Endangering the environment. Ruining our national heritage. Stick that sort of mud on a public figure and it'll soon finish his career."

I put my glass down on the table. I was trembling so much with agitation that I nearly spilt the drink. Was Brent making a harmless generalization or could I possibly have told him something about Barry—either just now or on the previous occasions when I had spoken of him? I could no longer remember what I had said. The past, the present, and the timeless world of the imagination were all inextricably mixed up together. This is senility, I thought, and yet I am too young for that so I must indeed be going mad.

"Are you all right?" asked Brent solicitously.

So my nervousness had been obvious. But I must not let him see that it had anything to do with what he had just said.

I blinked and looked at him in a dazed way.

"I'm sorry," I said. "I'm afraid I've been miles away. I suddenly thought of something—you know how it is when inspiration strikes. What were we talking about?"

"How to ruin a man's career," he said brightly.

"Oh yes." I put a hand to my head and frowned. "I was reminiscing about Barry, wasn't I. I do hope I haven't been boring you to death."

"No. I was interested."

It was impossible to tell from his manner whether or not I had said anything dangerously indiscreet.

"Shall we be moving?" I said, draining my glass. "It's getting rather late."

My fears receded as soon as we were back on the road and I encouraged Brent in the most reckless driving. We chose carpets and curtains at Harrods, pottered in and out of antique shops in Chelsea, and ended up in Piccadilly with Brent choosing himself a suit.

"It isn't happening," he kept saying. "It just is not happening. We've got into one of those nineteen-thirties films."

"Not 'thirties," I protested. "I'm not all that old. Come on—what theatre are we going to?"

We drove home in silence after the theatre, through the lovely limpid summer night, and drew up at Regency Terrace about one in the morning.

"Hadn't we better get the stuff out of the car now?" asked Brent.

I had already lost interest in the lampshades and the mirrors and the other bits and pieces that we had brought back with us and didn't care in the least if they were stolen. It would only mean that we could have the whole excursion over again.

"They'll be all right," I said yawning. "We'll unload in the morning."

"But don't we have to return the car?"

Damn the boy, I said to myself, with his petty, niggling shopkeeper's mind; no wonder he can't write another novel or sustain the possession of wealth and fame; he's quite incapable of thinking big.

"I'm buying the car," I said. "You can fix up the insurance tomorrow. It'll be in your name."

His yelp of ecstasy sounded very loud in the silence of the night. A light went on in the house next door.

"You've woken Mr. Thorburn," I said, half-laughing, half-reproachful.

"As long as it isn't Mrs. S.," he whispered.

My whole house was in darkness. I touched the switch inside the front door. The hall looked unfamiliar, as if we had wandered into somebody else's home. It felt as if we had been away for years.

'Ssh." I held up a warning finger and crept silently to the door of Mrs. Simmonds's room.

"I can hear her snoring," I said. "Would you believe it?" He suppressed a giggle.

"Good night, then," I said. "See you tomorrow."

He was leaning against the open front door. I moved towards him; the hall was like a brightly lit stage against the darkness of the night. I held out my hand and he raised it to his lips.

"What a treat for anyone who happens to be passing by!" I said mockingly.

"Oh Helen, I don't know how—I don't know how—"

"Go away and write it down in your novel," I said, shutting the door on him.

6

That night I dreamed of Brent, a deeply sensuous dream, from which I awoke exhausted but heavily satisfied. What a strange faculty of the human creature, this power of the imagination to produce physical sensations! But very profitable for the purveyors of pornography. Judging by myself, I thought, they ought to find as good a market among dirty old women as among dirty old men. But perhaps I was in a minority, or perhaps I was ahead of my time and it would take a generation or two of sexually conscious women to achieve this particular degree of equality with the male and to have their needs catered for in this particular way.

I yawned, stretched, and then sank back luxuriously on to the comfort of foam rubber and down pillow. The dream was still with me, its afterglow co-existing with my rational thoughts. A few weeks ago I would have been conscious only of the latter, my strongest physical sensations being those induced by apprehension or anxiety. The phobia had gone but other fears had taken its place—fear of losing control of myself, of saying things I ought not to say.

And, of course, the fear of losing Brent.

There was a knock at the door.

"Come in," I called lazily.

Mrs. Simmonds, in the pink crimplene suit which, like all her clothes, was a trifle too small for her, stumped in with a loaded tray.

"I've brought you breakfast," she said accusingly, "and I've left it late because you were so late back last night."

"Oh, thank you. That's so thoughtful of you," I gushed.

"Are you going to be very busy today," she went on, "or will there be any time to speak to you privately?"

She stood by the door, one hand on the knob, "looking volumes," as they say.

"Why don't you sit down and talk to me now?" I replied. "If you don't mind listening to me crunching toast."

She looked disconcerted. It is perhaps a little embarrassing to deliver an ultimatum to an employer who is lounging in bed. Rather like trying to fight a duel with somebody who insists on propping himself up against a tree.

"Do sit down," I repeated. "Have you had your breakfast? Or will you share my coffee?"

"I've had it, thanks," she said sulkily.

Poor Mrs. Simmonds. She was beaten from the start. She was horribly jealous all round; Brent had supplanted her with me and I had supplanted—if that is the right term for such an abortive relationship—her with him. We no longer had any cosy evening chats, and all the little details of converting the basement flat, which had it not been for Brent I would naturally have discussed with her, were being kept secret from her. Of course I was giving her wonderful food for gossip, and no doubt she was making a good meal of it, but this was not the most important. Her special relationship with me was no more; her self-esteem was badly hurt.

"I hope we didn't disturb you last night," I said. "I came in as quietly as I could."

"How long is this going on?" she asked abruptly. "I mean, I'm hardly earning my keep at the moment. I don't feel I'm being any use to you at all, with your being out so much. I wouldn't want you to feel you'd got to keep me on, Miss Mitchell, if you decide that you no longer need me here. But if you *have* got other plans I should be very glad to know. I mean, I shall have to make other arrangements, of course, and it may take time . . ."

Her voice trailed away. To sound reproachful and at the same time respectful, to extract from me a firm enough statement to satisfy her curiosity and at the same time not take any irrevocable step—this was too much for her ingenuity.

"I quite understand your position, Mrs. Simmonds," I said soothingly. I had no desire to torment the poor woman but on the other hand I did want her out of the way before I moved Brent into the basement flat.

"Perhaps it might be best if you were to look around for another job," I went on. "My plans are still a little vague, but I am thinking of going abroad for a while, and I may well spend long periods out of this country in future. In that case I shall shut up this house and put the basement flat in the hands of agents."

"And what about Mr. Ashwood?"

It burst out of her before she could stop herself.

"He has been extremely useful," I said. "I should never have got it all done without his help. I'm afraid it has rather held up his own work, though."

"Is he writing another book, then?"

"I believe so. There does seem to be a chance that my experiment will succeed."

Mrs. Simmonds looked somewhat placated at being thus taken into my confidence again. I pursued my advantage.

"I'm afraid he is becoming rather too dependent on me, however, and that is one of the reasons why I am planning to go away for a while. After all, there is nothing to hold me here, and I have gone very stale in my own writing and could do with a break."

This also went down well, and Mrs. Simmonds asked where I was going.

"To Germany—the Black Forest region," I replied, this being the first thing that came into my head. "I spent some very happy weeks there not long after the war and I should like to re-visit the area."

I was astonished at the conviction with which I spoke, considering that I had only invented this trip on the spur of the moment. Then my story-telling powers took over and I elaborated the scheme, explaining that I would be looking for local colour, and that there were a number of writers, publishers, and others whom I could call on when I was there. But it wasn't quite real; it was as if the plot of a book I was writing necessitated the removal of one of the characters for a while and the solution was a working holiday.

Mrs. Simmonds said that she had felt for a long time that

I was overworking and that I badly needed a break. This remark was the cue for me to reiterate the recuperative nature of my journey and we decided together that it was particularly important, at my time of life, not to get into a rut.

"So if you hear of any permanent post that might suit you," I said eventually, "don't hesitate to accept. I can manage with temporary help for a few weeks if necessary."

Exit Mrs. Simmonds, I said to myself when she had left the room. There would be a few odd ends to tie up, but for all intents and purposes I had written her out of the plot. It was rather like *Ten Little Niggers*—Marian, Mrs. Simmonds, who would be the next?

I told Brent of this fanciful notion of mine.

"How about the old chap next door?" he asked.

"Mr. Thorburn? Possibly. Although he can scarcely be said to be *in* the plot yet. That lunch with him the other day was the biggest non-event I have attended in years."

"What about me, then?"

We had stored our previous day's purchases in the big cupboard in the hallway of the basement flat and were sitting on the window-seat in the front room, waiting for the plumber to arrive.

"Oh no, not you, Brent. You will be the last to go. You will outstay them all."

He looked at me curiously. "You know, Helen," he said, "sometimes you frighten me."

"Good heavens! Why on earth do you say that?"

He wriggled about, gripping the edge of the window-seat and swinging his legs against the stripped plaster of the wall.

"Sometimes I feel you don't see people as people at all but as chessmen—pieces to be placed in the right position to use in the development of the story. Oh, I know I ought not to be saying this! After all you're doing for me, and deliberately letting me use you as the basis for a book—well, I ought to be saying thank you the whole time instead of criticizing you. But I can't help wondering why—I mean, what do *you* get out of it? I suppose you can watch me at close quarters and draw a character from me in a different way than you might have done otherwise, but I wouldn't have thought a novelist of your experience would have needed to do that.

So it must be an experiment, as you said. Experimenting with our lives. Your life, my life.''

He jumped up from the window-seat and began to move about the empty room, waving his arms about and getting more and more excited.

''I ought not to complain because I'm getting a hell of a lot out of it, and I can't draw back because it looks as if my new novel might be getting somewhere, but at the same time I can't help feeling—oh God, I don't know. Uneasy, I suppose. Like Cinderella coming up for the stroke of midnight. Or as if I was a puppet on a string.''

He stopped in front of me and called up the desperate look into his eyes.

''Are you doing all this to watch my reactions? Because if so then I think I'd rather not. I mean I know I'm not exactly an estimable character but there are limits. I mean even if I haven't stuck to one woman, at least it was genuine at the time and we weren't just using each other. I mean if you really are manipulating people in real life just to see how they behave then I can't help feeling it's rather horrible and cold-blooded.''

It was all I could do not to laugh, so incredible did it seem to me that he could be unaware of my feelings towards him— a young man with his experience and with his vanity. What a tribute to my self-control, that I had not given myself away; and how enormously thick must be the armour of my literary reputation, to protect me against the suspicion of having human failings like any other rich and lonely middle-aged woman.

There was no doubt as to his sincerity. His misunderstanding was totally in character. It was the magnitude of the favours I was heaping on him that had led him astray. Had they been on a smaller scale, he would have attributed them to the successful operation of his charm, but for all his egoism he did not lay a very high material value on himself. It was not modesty; it was a sign of his petty nature. He was a small-time exploiter and would never be anything else.

''My dear Brent,'' I said coolly, ''you really have got hold of the wrong end of the stick. I am not trying to manipulate anybody and I am certainly not cold-blooded. I find your services very useful and I am glad to be of use to you. After all, you did ask for my help, didn't you? And you admit yourself that my suggestion was a good one and has brought you inspiration. I am absolutely longing to know what you have written and I feel it is very restrained of me not to beg you to let me read it. Surely I can have the pleasure of putting forward these rather fanciful notions of mine from time to time, without being accused of some subtle and deep-laid plot against your character?''

"I'm sorry," he muttered, turning away and kicking at the roll of floor-covering that awaited attention. "I'm not ungrateful, honestly. It's just that I feel as if I've got caught up in something outside my control—as if everything was predetermined, as if I wasn't myself at all but part of somebody else's dream. Like in Alice in Wonderland. Sounds daft, doesn't it?''

He looked up at me again, his eyes begging me to reassure him. Barry would never have spoken like that, I thought; Barry always had everybody and everything well under his control. I knew perfectly well that in falling in love with Brent I was trying to recapture my passion for Barry, but nonetheless I was disappointed. This boy Brent was so feeble, for all that he looked like a young lion. He'd never even have the guts to deceive me, cheat me, treat me badly. He was too full of deference and I was sick of deference. He was constantly pushing me back into being Helen Mitchell, novelist, again when all I wanted was to be swept off my feet.

"You're not somebody's dream, you're very solid," I said wearily. "You've got thoroughly involved in your book, that's all that's wrong with you."

"Do you feel like that too?" he cried. "As if what you are writing is more real than what you are living through?"

"Of course. Everyone who writes fiction has that sensation from time to time. So do the people who read it. Surely you became totally absorbed in writing Road Without End?''

"Oh yes," he replied, but I knew that he was lying, and that from now on he was going to pretend to states of mind that in fact he did not experience, all in order to prove that he was on a par with myself.

"Oh to hell with writing!" I exclaimed, getting up off the window-seat. "What's happened to that plumber? Go and phone him, Brent."

For the rest of the morning I was very brisk and employer-like, thinking up another job for him to do as soon as he had finished the last one, and at lunch-time I sent him away, saying I was quite worn out after the long day yesterday and was going to rest and that he must get on with his book. It was very painful to deprive myself of his company for the afternoon but the tactic paid off. The next day he was at his most charming and even began to experiment tentatively with endearments and caresses. We'll get there yet, I thought, without my having to make it too plain.

A few days later I said: "How do you feel about acting chauffeur?" and without waiting for a reply I embarked on an account of my scheme for a tour in Germany.

"I loathe the chores of buying tickets and seeing to luggage," I explained. "And I prefer going by road. We'd have a quiet week or two to start with, and then there are a number of people I should like to visit. And whom you might be interested in meeting too," I added, belatedly remembering that he too could claim an entry into the right circles as a representative of modern English fiction, and that it would probably be this aspect of my suggestion that would appeal to him most.

He jumped at the idea and then drew back a little.

"There's only one thing—Jean might not like it."

"Jean?" I echoed, momentarily at a loss.

Since coming to work for me Brent had scarcely mentioned his home life and I was only too glad to leave blank in my mind all his activities outside the hours we spent together. On one occasion I had rung his number a female voice had answered, but the line had been poor and I couldn't tell whether the speaker had been young or old. Some self-deceptive—or defensive—mechanism in my mind had instantly conjured up a picture of an elderly landlady or cleaning woman and I had left a message without experiencing any stabs of jealousy.

They came, belatedly, at this moment, together with the recollection of Brent's first tea-time visit, the details of which I had managed to forget. Jean—the waitress. The current girlfriend. The same name as Barry's first wife, who had stood in my way for so many years. A common enough name.

"Jean?" I said yet again, very vaguely, as if my mind was occupied with far more important thoughts and was having difficulty in focusing, but in reality I was drowning in jealous fury.

"Of course!" I exclaimed, as if light had suddenly broken. "How stupid of me. I hadn't thought. Does she very much dislike your going away? It would only be for a few weeks, you know."

He seemed to come to a decision. "I'll fix it," he said confidently. "Perhaps I can take her somewhere for a holiday later."

"Oh dear," I said, "now you have made me feel very guilty. Doesn't Jean approve of your working for me?"

"Oh no. I mean yes, of course she does. In fact I think she's a bit envious—she'd like such a chance herself."

"It's your fault, you know," I said quite sharply. "You never talk about her. No wonder I forgot to take her into account."

"Oh well." He looked embarrassed. "There's nothing much to say."

"Is she pretty?"

"Tolerable."

"Intelligent?"

"Not particularly."

"Kind-hearted? Affectionate? Generous? No—don't trouble to reply. Of course she is. She was keeping you going, wasn't she, when you were more or less broke?"

"Yes, but it's different now, thanks to you."

I turned my back on him, pretended to look for something among the papers on top of the desk, and made the most terrible grimaces in an effort to control myself. Twenty years ago I had frequently felt like this—murderously jealous, driven temporarily into complete helplessness by the violence of the urge to destroy. Of course it had never broken the bonds; I had seldom made any reproaches to Barry, let along physically attacked him. But in one of my books I had had a woman stab her lover and my sensations as I described the incident came back vividly to me at this moment. I had lived through it, experiencing the very feel of the resistance of the flesh to the plunging knife, while at the same time knowing myself to be safely remote.

I continued to search among the papers and the action brought a little sense of relief. I picked up a pen and it felt like a dagger, and the whole workings of my mind were suddenly lit up as by a flash of lightning: it *had* been my dagger, and I had used it to write instead of to stab Barry. It had been my safety valve. I put it back neatly in the pen-tray; gradually I was regaining my self-control.

"That letter from the accountant," I muttered. "What did I do with it?"

Brent came up to the desk and began to search alongside me.

"Ah, here it is!" I cried, and was relieved to hear how normal my voice sounded. "I'm sorry," I went on. "We were talking about something, weren't we?"

"Going to Germany," he said after a short pause.

"Oh yes. And how to break the news to Jean. Well now." I stopped, apparently reflecting, and then went on: "What's your flat like, Brent? Are you happy in it?"

It turned out that they weren't at all happy there. It was a very small, so-called luxury flat in a block full of wealthy retired couples who sneered at Jean and were always trying to find grounds for complaint against them both—they were making too much noise, they were leaving their swimsuits out on the balcony to dry—idiotic things like that. And the rent was enormous and if it hadn't been for this stroke of luck in coming to work for me he would have had to find somewhere cheaper, but what on earth could you find?

"That settles it," I said. "You shall have the basement flat. You'll be completely independent and you can pay me the full rent. It'll still be a lot less than you're paying now and I'm sure it's a much nicer flat, and after all, you've chosen all the decorations and furniture so it ought to suit you."

He began to protest that he hadn't been angling for this at all, that he'd never dreamed, and so on.

"D'you think Jean will like it?" I interrupted.

"Oh yes. She'll like it all right."

"That's settled then. As soon as it's ready you can move in. I shall be glad to have somebody in the place after Mrs. Simmonds leaves. I shan't replace her. I'll make do with daily help. It will be nice to have the place to myself. There are only two things I must insist on."

I paused. "Don't look so worried," I went on, "they are to your advantage. The first one is that we fix definite working hours for you and that outside these your time is your own. So you need not fear that I shall be for ever calling you up to replace an electric light bulb or some such triviality.''

"I wasn't worrying about that," he said sulkily.

"Oh yes, you were. The second thing is that you bring Jean to see me tomorrow and then leave us alone to make each other's acquaintance.''

This time he made a better show of concealing his unease. Jean would be delighted, but please would I try not to be too overwhelming, as she was rather shy and nervous, particularly with authors and people like that.

"I shall show her the flat as a prospective tenant," I said. "We shall both have very specific roles to play and I assure you I will not overstep mine.''

He began to thank me effusively but I knew that he was worried.

"Come on, let's get down to this correspondence," I said, cutting him short. Forced raptures do not make for interesting conversation at any time, and I was still feeling shaken from the intensity of my reaction to his mention of Jean. What I could not yet admit to myself was the fact that he was beginning to bore me. His mind ran in well-defined grooves, his behaviour consisted in the same set of tricks; his phony, faintly complaining voice always jarred on me. Yet the attraction was as violent as ever and the need to be with him was growing stronger and stronger every day.

7

Jean was rather a surprise. Knowing Brent's snobbishness and
his mixture of conceit and servility towards people whom he
was trying to impress, I had assumed that he would play
down the qualities of any humble person with whom he was
intimately connected. But she really was an insignificant
looking little thing—slight, dark, wearing a lemon-coloured
dress and stubby white summer shoes from a cheap chain
store. She had a nice hair and rather appealing brown eyes
and that was all.

And it was practically impossible to get a word out of her.
I showed her the flat, explained what work remained to be
done, and stated the rent—all without a single mention of
Brent or any indication that she was in any way associated
with him. She nodded and smiled and sometimes said "Yes"
and sometimes "Oh yes." Only once did we achieve something approaching an exchange of thoughts.

"I'll leave you to think it over, Miss—Miss Graves," I
said in conclusion.

Brent had told me her name, but until this moment it had
escaped me.

"It's Mrs. Graves," she murmured, looking up at me with
wide and frightened eyes, as if she was admitting to a crime.

"I beg your pardon," I said calmly. "Mrs. Graves."

She had been clutching a big white handbag with her left
hand throughout the interview; the fingers were tucked under
the wide strap in such a way that it was impossible to see

65

whether she wore a ring. We ascended the broad steps of the area slowly together. I glanced sideways at her. She was a little older, perhaps, than had appeared at first glance but it was difficult to imagine how she had ever managed to produce enough speech to acquire—and then presumably to lose—a husband. She was very nervous with me and presumably she behaved differently with Brent and her own friends, but I received not the faintest whiff of what that behaviour might be. She was a total blank to me, a character right outside my fictional range.

It was frustrating and at the same time rather intriguing. Unlike Brent, she was unpredictable and might have great potential.

"If you could let me know by Saturday," I said as we reached the top of the steps and stood blinking in the full glare of the noonday sun, "I should be grateful. I think it would suit you and I'm sure you will suit me, so I hope you will decide to take the flat."

"Oh yes," she said breathlessly, "it's a lovely flat. Thank you very much."

She stood trembling with the effort of having said so much, awaiting permission to depart.

I held out my hand.

"Goodbye then, Mrs. Graves. I hope we are soon going to be neighbors."

Her hand touched mine. It was surprisingly cold. The fingers drew together and slipped, snakelike, from my grasp.

"Goodbye, Miss Mitchell," she murmured, and scuttled away.

I came back to my front hall to find Mrs. Simmonds, pink and plump and bursting with curiosity, emerging from her own rooms.

"Oh," she said, "I thought I heard the laundry van."

"Did you see her?" I asked with faint malice. "She looks like being a quiet tenant. I wouldn't want the terrace to suffer from a lot of rave-up parties while I am away."

"I wish you'd let me stay on and look after the whole place for you," cried Mrs. Simmonds with a violence that seemed to surprise herself. "I've saved up quite a bit of money, you know. I wouldn't even mind staying without salary, provided it wasn't for too long—three or four months perhaps."

"But there would be nothing for you to do."

"I could take over the basement flat and pay you rent for it, and I could find myself a temporary job while you were away."

So it was out. She was more skilful than I had supposed and I had been premature in assuming that she had been written out of the story.

"It's an idea," I said slowly, as if I was really considering it, "but it's not fair on you. I may even suddenly decide to sell the house. I really would feel much happier if I knew you were comfortably settled in a permanent position."

"You'd like me to go ahead with my application, then?"

"Yes please. Has anything cropped up that appeals to you?"

"There's a possible job at the college, and another as housekeeper to a titled family who have recently bought a large estate in Sussex."

"That sounds right up your street," I said. Mrs. Simmonds was a great one for royal occasions and family trees and such matters.

"Yes, I think I should like it," she agreed, but a moment later she burst out again:

"I don't like leaving you, Miss Mitchell, and that's a fact. I'm worried about you. I ought not to be saying this, but I can't help it. I feel you need someone to look after you—someone you can really trust. I don't think you realize just how wicked people can be. Oh yes, I know you *write* about them doing the most dreadful things, but that's quite a different matter. You can make your characters do what *you* want, can't you? But you just can't do that in real life. You know, I've worked a lot among clever people and they are all so helpless—so easily cheated and taken in. I'd hate to think that anybody—I mean, you are so kind and generous and always wanting to help people and to see the best in them. And we've always got on well together, haven't we? I've never intruded or anything, and it's not the money or the comfort that matters, but I've really *liked* working for you, and I can't help worrying—"

She stopped abruptly. Her face was puckered and redder than ever. She was very nearly in tears.

I was touched. She sounded absolutely sincere and I could

not remember the last time when somebody had genuinely considered my welfare without thought of what they were going to receive in return. Even Marian's friendship, I now began to perceive, had not been what I thought it was. I thanked Mrs. Simmonds very warmly and assured her that I knew perfectly well what I was doing.

"I see I shall have to take you into my confidence," I said, and I explained to her the relationship between Jean Graves and Brent. "It's in the nature of a literary experiment," I concluded. "You know his problem and my attempts to solve it? I can't just leave him in the lurch now, so I have another plan in mind. I don't know what will happen and I'm afraid I can't explain it in detail, but I do promise you that any actions of mine that seem a little unusual are in fact motivated purely by the instinct of research."

I watched Mrs. Simmonds closely as I spoke. Would this explanation sound as unconvincing to her as it did to myself? Or would she be taken in by a lot of learned-sounding rigmarole?

"Well, I suppose if it's really a matter of your wanting to make use of him for your next book," she began grudgingly.

"It is indeed," I said firmly. "One tends to get out of touch with how younger people think and feel. It's high time I refreshed myself in this respect."

She seemed to see the force of this argument. "But there are plenty of nice decent young people around," she added.

"Ah yes, my dear Mrs. Simmonds," I said, "that's just the point. I don't want nice decent people for my stories, I want nasty ones."

"Oh." She was taken aback. "Oh. I suppose so."

"And I want to know exactly how they behave when they scent the possibility of turning something to their advantage, just how far they are prepared to go. Naturally there are some risks in this experiment, but you never get anything if you aren't prepared to take a risk."

I continued to talk on these lines for a few minutes more, with Mrs. Simmonds now listening submissively. It was tiresome to be obliged to labour at arguments that I knew to be faulty and I found myself longing for her to be gone. The little uprush of kindly feelings towards her had trickled away and I saw her only as an obstacle in my path, a nagging

reminder of what one part of myself knew I ought to do—
stop playing with fire, get rid of Brent before it was too late.

But I could not get rid of Brent. He alone could fill the
vacuum that had been caused by the sudden drying up of my
creative flood. His presence alone—stirring up long-
suppressed physical yearnings, jealousies, torrents of sensation both pleasant and unpleasant—could give me relief.

8

It had now become widely known among my literary acquaintances that Brent was acting as my secretary, and considerable speculation was going on as to whether this was the only service he was performing. This rather gave me satisfaction and I encouraged the rumours whenever I had a chance. On one occasion an item appeared in a widely read gossip column to the effect that Brent and I were "collaborating" on an experimental novel, with a hint that the collaboration might be of a more permanent nature. This produced quite a buzz of interest and a number of telephone calls, most of which I dealt with noncommittally. Three of the reactions to this item did, however, affect me more nearly.

The first was a conversation with Marian.

"I see you're determined to make a fool of yourself," she began.

I taxed her with envy of my position and went on to say some unforgivable things. How blind I had been, I said, not to have realized that she herself had been hopelessly in love with Barry all through those frenzied years; that was why she had stuck to me, to feel herself still in touch with him. No wonder she had wanted me to marry the worthy Geoff; she saw herself as my successor with Barry, consoling him for losing me; at first a sympathetic listener, she would later become his indispensable aide.

"Really, Helen, I think you are going out of your mind," said Marian harshly. "I never heard such a fantastic array of nonsense in my life. It's a pity you can't restrain your morbid imagination to within the pages of your books.''

''Forget it,'' I said wearily. Her last remark had aroused these disturbing fears of mine again. ''I expect I am making it all up, as you say. Forget all about it. And about me too.''

She started to climb down then but the conversation had left a very unpleasant taste.

The second outcome of the gossip item had its pleasurable aspects. It was a quarrel with Brent. He was deeply offended at the idea that we were collaborating on a novel. It was a great blow to his conceit to descend from the heights of sole authordom and to play second fiddle to me, and he accused me of starting the rumour.

''Forget it,'' I said in much the same tones as I had used to Marian. ''Everyone else will in a day or two.''

''But it's simply not true. You said you didn't want to see my novel. You've had nothing to do with the writing of it. It's intolerable to have everyone saying that you're writing it for me. Collaborations! With a name like yours! Everyone knows what *that* means.''

I let him fume for some time. The voice was becoming more and more disagreeable—slipping from mid-Atlantic to its original Cockney and then back again—but he looked wonderful, stamping around the room, banging things down on the desk, a taut and nervous mass of flesh and muscle and bone. I'll get him thoroughly worked up, I thought, and make him say some very unkind things. Then I shall gradually show him how wrong and how ungrateful he is. He will feel very guilty. We shall have some grovelling apologies and conclude with another delightful reconciliation scene.

All went according to plan and the scene ended with a very satisfactory embrace.

The third reaction to the rumour was the most distressing. This was a visit from my brother Philip. Normally such events took place only three times a year—at Christmas, in spring during our local arts festival when we went to a concert together, and in October on the anniversary of our parents' death. They were killed in an air raid in the Second World War and our younger brother, Oliver, was reported missing in the Far East shortly afterwards. Philip himself was back from North Africa, recovering from dysentery and a leg wound that left him permanently lame, and I was in a state of general disenchantment and indecision at the time, disliking the school at which I was teaching and longing for somebody or something—apart from the war effort—to which to devote my life. I had not yet met Barry.

It must have been a very bad time, but all that I retained in my memory from those days was a vivid little picture of a ward in Charing Cross Hospital—Phil's face against the pillows, distorted with the pain of an anxious, repressed character who can find no outlet for emotion; myself standing helplessly at the side of the bed, tall, gawky, unappealing in the fashions and hair-style of the time; and a perky little ginger-haired nurse whose trite expressions of sympathy broke into our frozen misery and who later took advantage of Phil's desperate need for comfort by getting engaged to him.

Their marriage turned out well enough in its way, with Dora dictating their exact mode of living at every stage, culminating in the triumphant acquisition of a uniquely desirable residence in the Surrey stockbroker belt and minor public schools for the two boys.

I always found them a depressing family and wondered if things would have been different if my parents and Oliver had lived. Probably not. Some girl or other was bound to seize on the possibility of converting Phil's conscientious and hardworking intelligence into a nice fat bank account. As a child he would dream over the great cases of Marshall Hall and picture himself on the judge's bench: as an adult he sat all day in a rabbit warren of an office block, telling rich people how to get rid of their husbands or wives without having to contribute too much towards the upkeep of their discarded children.

A sad fate. Not only did he have to satisfy, but he also had to be the mouthpiece of an Ideal Consumer in our insanely acquisitive and materialistic society. Probably he had not been allowed to have a thought of his own for years.

I was alone when Mrs. Simmonds showed him up, since Brent was down in the basement flat attending to the laying of carpets.

"This is a surprise!" I exclaimed. "Where's Dora?"

"I dropped her off to do some shopping. She'll be along in about an hour. Would it be convenient to give us lunch or shall we all go to a hotel? I hope you're free," he added as an afterthought.

I instructed Mrs. Simmonds to prepare a meal for three. It was disappointing to have to forego my usual tête-à-tête lunch with Brent, but clearly this was an occasion that would have to be faced sooner or later.

"You're lucky to find me here," I said. "I'm going away as soon as the basement flat is finished."

I told the now familiar story, omitting only to state that Brent was coming with me, and Philip listened without much interest, moving first, as he always did, to our father's old desk, and then sitting down on one of the dining-chairs. I broke into my eulogy of the Bavarian scenery to ask if his leg was troubling him.

"Yes," he replied brusquely.

"I'm sorry," I said.

We were silent for a moment.

"How are the boys?" I asked next.

"The boys" were in fact both very prosperous young executives in some vast corporation—oil or chemicals, I could never remember which. They had both made the right sort of marriage and acquired the right sort of house at a much earlier age than their father did and I could not imagine what they would do with the next thirty or forty years of their lives. More and more of the same thing, presumably. And their children would start with an even bigger bonus, and so on ad infinitum down the generations.

I scarcely listened to Philip's reply. I was suddenly assailed by a wave of nostalgia that almost took my breath away.

"We had the best of it after all, Phil," I cried. "With all we lost and all we went through—at least we had a childhood that was not stifled with possessions and strangled with the fear of losing them. At least as kids we still had room to breathe and hope and dream."

He looked at me blankly through his cautiously trendy horn-rimmed spectacles. Dora's choice. His hair seemed a lot greyer than on the previous visit only a few months ago. Perhaps if he had responded to my outburst and we could really have communicated with each other I might have been diverted from the course on which I was set, but he was never a creature of impulse and it was too much to expect him

suddenly to admit the long-drawn-out futility of his life. Besides, he was there for a purpose. Dora expected him to inherit my money—I being the elder. For years there had
seemed no danger that I might marry or make a will in anybody else's favour. They knew that my personal life was a
vacuum. But the rumours about my association with Brent
had evidently worried Dora and she had decided that it needed
investigating. Philip had been sent on ahead to spy out the
land and try to soften me up before the concerted attack. But
he wasn't making much headway; he was reluctant to tackle
me and he was tired from the drive and from the incessant
little nagging of pain.

I poured him some whiskey and steeled myself against the
invasions of pity. Blood might be thicker than water but it
was still a very poor defence against the single-minded on-
slaughts of human greed.

"We saw the bit about you in the paper," he said presently. "We were rather surprised to see you had taken on a
protégé."

I did not reply. I was filled with revulsion. This was a
scene that I did not even want to write, still less to live
through. My poor little brother, trying to get us to play law-
courts in the nursery at the old rectory: oh do be a witness,
Nell! It's my turn now. You and Oliver always have longer at
your things than I do at mine!

No, I was not going to play Dora's game now. Let her do
her own dirty work.

"Brent's downstairs at the moment," I said, "attending to
all the chores that bore me stiff. Would you like to meet him
and see the flat? If you can manage the stairs, that is."

He fell for the temptation. Dora would surely forgive him
for taking the opportunity to inspect the enemy. I introduced
him to Brent, but in all the confusion of carpet-laying and
curtain-hanging that was going on they neither of them had
much chance to sum up the other. And I myself kept up a
non-stop running commentary, giving Brent instructions in a
very businesslike manner and making it very plain to him
that he was a paid employee and not one of the family on
this occasion. That served the double purpose of hurting his
pride and providing scope for another reconciliation scene,

and of throwing dust in Philip's eyes with regard to my feeling for Brent.

When we came back upstairs Philip accepted another drink and said quite amicably:

"Seems a decent enough lad. Shall you continue to make use of him once the flat is in order?"

"It depends," I replied, "on what there is to do and whether he is willing to spare the time."

This answer was well received and I even began to hope that we might be able to dispense with the family protest scene altogether. But Philip was frowning over a train of thought of his own.

"Who is it?" he muttered. "Who is it the fellow reminds me of? Very strong resemblance—same build, same colouring—oh yes, of course. Barry Walters. In his younger days, of course."

I could feel the blood rush to my cheeks and I sat down hastily. So the scene was to be included after all, but in a rather different form that I had expected. I could not speak; it was not yet clear to me what I was going to say.

Philip drained his glass and glanced at me somewhat apprehensively.

"Sorry, Nell," he said. "Didn't mean to upset you. It just came out."

"You don't upset me in the least. And now you mention it, I do see some resemblance."

"Doing very well, isn't he? Barry, I mean. I read the other day that he had bought a period house somewhere in this part of the country. Fifteen rooms and twenty acres of ground—that must have cost him a pretty penny."

"I expect so," I said, entwining my fingers together. Some strong emotion was stirring within me, taking possession of the muscles of my hands, endowing them with unusual force—the force to crush and hurt.

But it was not my poor brother, drooling along on the lines that his wife had laid down for him, who was the object of this sudden craving to torment and destroy.

"Pity things turned out as they did," continued Philip, sadly shaking his head.

"How do you mean?"

"If only you could have—"

He broke off and again peered at me anxiously. Philip
didn't know quite as much as Marian did about my long affair
with Barry but he knew the essence of it, and he harboured
a grudge against me for a different reason: he could not forgive me for not arranging to become Barry's wife after his
first wife's death. That, in Philip's view—which of course was
Dora's—would have put everything right. The shame of having a sister involved in an adulterous affair would have been
gloriously cancelled out had that sister acquired the lawful
title of Lady Walters. Such an asset for the family—far more
satisfactory than being closely related to Helen Mitchell, novelist. The latter, for all her prestige, was inevitably a somewhat controversial figure, but Lady Walters would have been
above suspicion, no dangerously independent female, but a
pale and virtuous appendage of her husband—a relative to be
spoken of with unadulterated pleasure in any company.

"He happened to have a wife already," I said as calmly
as I could.

"But after she died—"

"He was already deeply committed to the present Lady
Walters."

"Good lord, I never knew. You don't mean that she was
expecting—I thought they had no children."

"You thought right. What I meant was that he never asked
me."

"Good God! You mean to say—after all those years—and
all you did for him—you mean that he'd got another woman
in tow?"

I nodded. My hands were less restless now. Philip's indignation seemed to be absorbing my own passionate anger and
I could not help but be touched that for the first time for
many years he was speaking with his own voice and not that
of his wife.

"It's preposterous!" he exploded. "Why ever didn't you
tell me this before, Nell?"

"Pride, I suppose," I said wearily. "Anyway, I'd have
made him a rotten wife. I was far too full of conscientious
scruples."

"Nonsense. You'd have been the making of him."

"He's not done all that badly without me, has he?"

"He'd have done even better with your help."

"No, my dear, that's where you are wrong. I should have been his undoing."

As I spoke my eyes turned to the desk. I was attacked by an overwhelming desire to unlock the top drawer, take out the notebooks that contained my diary, and let Philip read the entries for those critical days before Barry and I parted for ever. It would be the first time another human eye had ever seen them—those tortured outpourings recording the struggle of conscience versus love, which was to culminate in an uneasy compromise. It would be interesting to know whether those entries constituted any sort of valid evidence of Barry's behaviour—a point that had never occurred to me before. I had never understood the details of the case; that would have required a minute knowledge of the workings of the government office in question, but the gist of it had been only too brutally clear. That Barry should think I would approve—that was one of the most hurtful aspects of it all.

"So what it amounts to," I had recorded myself as saying, "is that you in your position of Planning Minister are giving permission for a huge tract of the most beautiful natural scenery in England to be destroyed by this monstrous fun-fair in return for a big share of the profits."

The essence of his reply had been that it was an exciting new development and that even the preservationists would love it once they got used to it, and that in any case it could never be traced that he had received any material benefit from it and that everybody would soon forget that it had been authorized at the time when he was in office.

He had been right about the last two items of his argument, wrong about the first two.

But Philip was talking again.

"I'm sorry he behaved so badly towards you, Nell, and I can't say I ever liked him personally. But one has to admit that he's done a great deal to preserve what is left of our countryside. And it looks as if he is really going to tackle that appalling People's Park question. Madness—ever to let it be built. It was bound to become an absolute hotbed of drug-pushing and crime of all sorts. However, if anyone can do anything about it, I'm sure Barry Walters is the man."

I stared at my brother in amazement. Obviously he had not the least suspicion of Barry's integrity. He wasn't stupid, and he did not live remote from the world. His opinion of Barry was no doubt shared by countless other people of moderate honesty and goodwill. The impulse to show Philip the entries in my diary died away. In view of what I had just told him he would probably regard the diary as the hysterical fabrication of a jilted and resentful woman.

Anyway it was all old history, as dead as last week's meals—swallowed, digested, and excreted. It would serve no public purpose to expose Barry now. He had made a nasty mess and he would clear it up again. The natural course of human history—to create muddles and then to put them right. And as for myself, it would have been just the same had he been as virtuous as his present image. I would never have married him; desire had already died before that final quarrel. Curious, that it had taken me fifteen years to realize that.

"Yes," I said to Philip, "I expect Barry will manage to get the place closed down."

The subject was at an end. Our drawing together had been very shortlived. Carefully and efficiently we manoeuvred ourselves apart again, talking about the weather and the state of the traffic on the London road. Dora would be arriving any moment now and it was advisable not to have any abrupt and obvious change of conversation when she entered the room.

In fact the lunch was less of an ordeal than I had expected. I excused myself for a few minutes beforehand, pretending I had a telephone call to make. This gave Philip the opportunity to report to his wife concerning my relationship with Brent. Evidently the report was satisfactory, for Dora was quite gracious to me throughout the meal, asking with particular interest about the royalties on my last book, and beaming on me when I agreed with her that running a big house nowadays was a very expensive business indeed.

It was only after they had gone that I found myself overcome with profound depression—an intolerable loathing of all the ways of this world and all the people in it, that was even worse than the condition of non-feeling plus obsessional wordspinning from which Brent had rescued me. I sat in front of the desk with the key to the long drawer lying in the palm of my hand. It was in my mind to take out those diaries and burn them. Mrs. Simmonds was out for the evening and nobody else was expected. Occasionally I had a log fire to supplement the radiators and it would be a simple matter to set a light to the diaries in the wide grate and clear out the ashes myself.

I must have sat there an hour or more in total lethargy, incapable of action. In the end I replaced the key in the small drawer in the top part of the desk, where it was always kept, and went to bed.

9

Morning brought a renewal of hope and two firm decisions. The first was to find some excuse for cancelling Philip's next few visits and the second was to hasten on the departure for Germany.

"I want to get away next week," I told Mrs. Simmonds. "I'll pay your hotel bills until you get fixed up elsewhere. But I must shut up this house before I go."

The idea of shutting up the house had become an obsession with me. It seemed to symbolize the end of a prison sentence—fifteen years of remorseless mental activity that had followed on the death of the heart.

I had bought the house as a duty rather than as a pleasure. Helen Mitchell—rising star in the literary firmament—needed a worldly base from which to shine forth, and it had served its purpose as an elegant casing for the machine. But apart from my father's old desk, which still retained an aura of the eagerness and innocence of childhood, none of the contents had any sentimental value for me and I didn't care if I never saw them again. In fact I could not visualize my return at all. It was as if the house was going to dissolve and disappear during my absence, like the setting for a novel or the scene of a play that ceases to exist when it has served its turn.

Brent and Jean moved into the basement flat. I gave them both keys to the upper part of the house and Jean offered to forward my mail and water the plants during my absence. At this point Mrs. Simmonds was moved to make another protest. She had grasped by now that I intended to take Brent with me and she was apparently resigned to my making a fool of myself over him. What was worrying her most was the fact that I knew nothing whatever about Jean, had no guarantee even as to her basic honesty, and yet was proposing to leave her in a position of trust that I had denied to Mrs. Simmonds herself.

"All right then," I said wearily. "Stay on here yourself if you must. Fix it between yourself and Mrs. Graves. I don't care who does what—I just don't want to have to think about it. And hand your key to Mr. Thorburn when you finally go. He has been pestering me with requests to attend to my interests during my absence and that ought to shut him up."

Mrs. Simmonds brightened up a little at the mention of Mr. Thorburn and suggested that he should be invited in before I went away so that he could take a good look round the house and see that everything was in order.

"So you think Mrs. Graves is planning to steal the silver," I said. "I suppose there is no hope of convincing you that I don't care a damn if she does?"

"Oughtn't we to lock up the best pieces?" countered Mrs. Simmonds.

"Do what you like!" I shouted. "I don't care, I tell you. I don't care if the whole place is stripped or burned to the ground. I simply don't *care*."

She stared at me as if I had gone out of my mind.

"It's such a pity," she said, "that you aren't going with Miss Gray or somebody else who would look after you."

"If I need a nurse I can hire one."

She glared at me and left the room and for the next few days we were barely on speaking terms.

But on the Saturday morning before the Monday on which Brent and I were due to depart, Mrs. Simmonds came up to my drawing-room with a letter in her hand, obviously bursting with good news.

"I've got the job!" she cried.

"Congratulations. Which one?"

"At Charlesworth Hall. It's a big estate near Lewes." Her voice took on a respectful tone. "Much of the time it will only be catering for the family, since they have bought the house as a country retreat, but I gather that there will be a certain amount of entertaining to be done—people in the Government, you know—and I shall have a staff of three on these occasions."

"Just a minute," I said, "I'm all at sea. I don't remember writing you any references for a big country house."

"Oh, didn't I tell you? I heard of it through that new agency in the Queen's Road—they have all the best appointments. I went for an interview last Wednesday."

She had not told me. That had been one of the days when we had not spoken.

"Sit down and tell me all about it now," I said.

She held out the letter for me to read, but even before my eyes caught sight of the letterhead and the signature I knew its authorship. The sensation of having been here before was strong within me and so too was the feeling of doom, of a story inexorably taking its course. It was as if my imagination, instead of plotting novels, was planning the course of my life and I had no control over it.

I ran my fingers over the thickly embossed letterhead. The address was Barry's flat in Westminster. So he still kept it on. It was not a particularly luxurious apartment—in the days when I had visited him there his annual income had not yet reached five digits—but of course it was very conveniently situated.

"Dear Mrs. Simmonds," I read, "my husband and I are very pleased to offer you the post of resident housekeeper at Charlesworth Hall on the terms that we discussed with you this afternoon."

There followed details of accommodation, hours of work and salary—this last being no greater than the sum paid by myself. I wondered that he had not offered more, since in any case it would be paid out of public money. Barry's extraordinary ingenuity in arranging for his living expenses to be paid for by the taxpayer was a characteristic that had always distressed me, daughter of a poor parson that I was, and it had been the cause of many an argument that I invariably lost. It was not that my passion for him had clouded my judgment; there had never been one moment when I had not seen him, ice-clear, as the plausible rogue that he was; when I had not been aware of every little meanness, every shifty or greedy action. But apart from his overwhelming attraction for me he did have one big positive quality, and that was imagination. While he was capable of pettiness, he was also capable of "thinking big." There was nothing too vast or too complicated for his mind to seize on; he did things on a grand scale. He would have made an equally good job of being a super-criminal as he was now of presenting himself as the hero of the preserve-our-planet lobby.

All this went through my mind as I read Lady Walters's letter to Mrs. Simmonds, taking rather longer over it than was necessary.

"Well," I said, looking up at her at last and handing her back the letter, "this is a surprise. But I am delighted for your sake. It sounds exactly what you want and should bring you in touch with all sorts of interesting people."

She agreed enthusiastically and went on:

"I believe it was because I had worked for you that I got the job. They both interviewed me—Lord Walters too—and when I said I had been with you for five years he was very interested and said that was the highest possible recommendation. I believe he said that he had had the honour of meeting you—something like that."

She looked at me curiously. I had command of my features again now and could return her look. Peers of the realm—even life peers—whose activities were well publicized, evidently took precedence over well-known lady novelists in Mrs. Simmonds's social hierarchy. She had, however, awarded me a little reflected glory and my stock, which had been rapidly diminishing since I had taken up with Brent, was somewhat raised by this remark of Barry's.

"I became acquainted with him over some work I was engaged in at one time," I said, "before I devoted all my energies to writing novels. We lost touch when the job came to an end and I have never met the present Lady Walters. Did you find her agreeable?"

Mrs. Simmonds answered with modified rapture but I did not pay much attention to what she said. My mind was roaming back again over the years. Rita Rendall she had been then. It was true that I had never met her, but I had heard a lot about her from people who for one reason or another were interested in driving a wedge between Barry and myself. She worked for a typing agency and became a frequent visitor at the Westminster flat. All he ever said about her was that she was "quite useful" and "very quick at picking up the essentials of the political scene." I derived the most reliable information about her from Jean Walters, Barry's first wife, my rival for so many years. A sad, defeated woman. My only consolation for the misery I must have caused her was that if it had not been me, it might well have been somebody who would have made her life even more intolerable. In the last months of her fatal illness a curious intimacy sprung up between us—we were sympathetic enemies, and it was then that she had told me about Rita Rendall.

"She's determined to marry him," she said. "She flatters him and makes eyes at him and he's getting to an age when a man likes that sort of thing."

This was something I had never been able to do and neither had Jean Walters. She would have hated the idea of Barry selling the permission to build the People's Park for whatever sum he got out of it, but Rita Rendall would have been delighted at his cleverness. On the other hand she would have been equally delighted to possess such a mighty hold over him and would not have hesitated to use it to gain her own ends.

"Lady Walters was very affable to me," Mrs. Simmonds was saying, "but I don't think one would want to get on the wrong side of her. I noticed that Lord Walters tended to defer to her."

So Rita Rendall had Barry under her thumb. Whether by threats, by nagging, or by making herself useful and keeping all rivals at a safe distance, she had achieved a position that would always have been beyond my powers.

I moved towards my desk, hoping that Mrs. Simmonds would take the hint and leave the room. The impulse to break out into telling the true story of Barry had come upon me again, even more strongly than when I had felt the urge to tell Philip. And with it was this pulsing fury, this mindless urge to destroy.

I had difficulty in removing the lid from the portable typewriter. I prodded at it, frowned at it, and heard myself saying:

"I am sure you will be able to cope with Lady Walters. I

hope you will be very happy there. Damn this typewriter! No, it's all right, thanks. I've got it off now.''

I sat down in the big swivel chair. I looked up at Mrs. Simmonds. She was suspended in nothingness—a pink reflection in moving water, the edges blurred and ever-changing. My lips moved again. The pinkness disappeared. I heard the slight click of the door closing. The fury died away but my arms felt like lead. I grasped the handles of the long drawer of the desk and pulled feebly. It did not shift. I had not the strength to reach up to the little drawer above where I kept the key. I slumped back and shut my eyes. There was a voice throbbing in my mind: you can't escape, it seemed to be saying; there's no way out; it is going to happen and you are powerless to stop it.

After a while I went to the telephone and rang Brent in the basement flat. It was Saturday morning, outside his working hours, and I had promised not to disturb him then, but this was an emergency.

"I want you to attempt the impossible," I said, "and move our car ferry booking forward to tomorrow. If they can't do it, then cancel and we'll hire a car the other side. The main thing is that we get away tomorrow and not on Monday."

I didn't ask whether it would be convenient for him and Jean. There was that in my voice that told him it would be useless to protest.

"Don't bother me with any of the details," I went on. "Just ring me back and let me know what you've arranged. Oh and by the way, if you and Jean would like to come up during the evening, I'm having a farewell party. Very informal. Just the usual crowd—as many as can come at such short notice. I'm phoning them now . . . no, it's all right . . . I can do it . . . you get on with the travel arrangements."

I cut him short and began an orgy of telephoning. Everybody who had ever attended one of Helen Mitchell's evening gatherings. My voice went on and on . . . "Sorry, it's such short notice . . . been very busy lately . . . may be away for some time . . . a sort of house-cooling party . . ."

When I had collected about twenty acceptances I called Mrs. Simmonds and explained. She was surprised but pleased. Evidently the hysterical despair that had driven me to this gesture was not showing in my face.

The party was a great success. I watched myself being
Helen Mitchell, hostess, with detached interest. A very cred-
itable farewell performance. Even the bouquets were not
lacking, for some of the guests had brought offerings of flow-
ers. I handed them to Mrs. Simmonds in the kitchen.

"Silly, isn't it," I said, "when they know I'm just about
to go away."

She buried her head in a bunch of roses the same colour
as her face.

"Lovely," she murmured.

"And these are for you, Jean," I said, turning to Jean
Graves who had constituted herself Mrs. Simmonds's assistant and was slipping in and out of the kitchen and handing
round refreshments with the self-effacing expertise of the
trained waitress.

She thanked me in her whispering voice and then turned
to Mrs. Simmonds for instructions as to what she should do
next. This obviously pleased Mrs. Simmonds, who seemed
to have suspended her suspicion of Jean for the time being.
The next thing, I thought, is that Mrs. S. will be taking Jean
along to Lord and Lady Walters as assistant housekeeper.

And that would leave Brent and me.

But the notion of having him to myself was beginning to
lose its savour. I wasn't even particularly looking forward to
our travels together now. It was the shutting the door of the
house that mattered; not the going somewhere else. Perhaps
after all the journey would not be necessary; perhaps there
was some other escape route waiting for Helen Mitchell.

All the evening, as I heard her making the expected
noises—cynicism laced with compassion—I was wondering
whether she was going to stand up and declaim the true story
of her life to everyone present, just as Brent had done on an
earlier occasion. Was she going to astonish her audience with
the facts that lay behind the carefully edited biographical note
that appeared on the publicity handouts? She was drinking
more than usual; she was actually talking about Lord and
Lady Walters, telling a couple of journalists that Mrs. Simmonds was going to be their housekeeper. General conversation about Lord Walters and pollution. General approval of
his activities. One or two dissident voices, but only on minor
matters. He'd been a bit abrupt with the anti-blood sport

lobby; he wasn't sufficiently in touch with the feelings of ordinary people—that sort of thing. But not the faintest hint of a suspicion that he was anything but incorruptible. Helen Mitchell reacted as she always did to such conversations; it was not the first time they had taken place in her drawing-room.

"Yes, it does look as if he is going to do something about that ghastly People's Park," she said with controlled approval.

I listened to her in amazement. How could she endure it? Now is the moment, I thought; that is why this party has been arranged, with all these news-hounds present, with Barry Walters well in the headlines; now is the moment to hit back, to take revenge for all those wasted years, this loveless life; now is the moment to strike the fatal blow.

But nothing happened. Helen Mitchell continued to do her act and I was sickened by her cowardice and hypocrisy.

The party went on very late. I left Brent and Jean and Mrs. Simmonds to clear up the débris, while I went to bed. Hour after hour passed in a semi-coma, with total loss of identity. Somewhere there was Helen Mitchell, novelist, thinking, writing, talking, doing her piece. And somewhere else was this swelling fury of destruction, its ambitions boundless, its object everything.

Towards morning—at least it seemed to be towards morning—there was an interval of clarity when the two parts merged and I knew exactly what I had to do. It was too late now to burn those diaries before I went away, and my journey would be no escape if I were to take them along with me in my overnight case. But there was time to make up a big parcel containing the diaries and the typescripts of the two unpublished novels, including the carbon copies, and write a covering note to my bank requesting that the contents of the parcel be placed in the safe until I sent further instructions. No post office open on Sunday, of course, but Mr. Evans was always up early arranging for the delivery of the Sunday papers, and he was a friendly soul who would gladly hold over the parcel till the Monday morning and dispatch it for me then.

My mind settled itself to concentrating on the operations

of packing, typing, and addressing, and directed these operations skilfully.

And then it relapsed into confusion again, and it was only the sight of Brent, yawning, somewhat bleary-eyed, but cheerful at the prospect of letting the big car loose on Continental motorways, that brought me safely back to time and place and circumstance.

INTERLUDE

10

After we had been a week in the little resort high up in the pine woods I began to realize just how mentally unbalanced I had been for months past. The very realization was a sign that the worst was over. Delirium does not know itself; it sees only the projections of the fevered imagination. For a long time I had been working up to the peak of delirium represented by my farewell party, but with that crisis behind me the return to normal was only a matter of time. It had indeed been a very sound instinct, underneath all the hysteria, that had told me to get away at once and seek recovery in different surroundings.

Brent spent most afternoons in the swimming-pool behind the hotel, while I sat on my balcony in front, gazing with the listless eye of convalescence at the waterfall and the long sweep of greensward sliced by the dark woods beyond. This time of solitude was very precious and I had not the least desire to watch him swim. We had become lovers rather as if carrying out a duty. His enthusiasm was obviously faked and as for myself, I was bored and with scarcely any feeling save a mild revulsion. So much for all my dreams of a renewal of life and a fresh ration of ecstasy. There was disappointment of course, but there was also an undercurrent of something like relief—relief at being spared an emotional enslavement to a person whom my mind despised.

I sat on the balcony and really rested for the first time in many years. I was neither mentally polishing up phrases nor

was I imagining an abandonment to passion. The future was
a blank and when I looked at the past it was to regard it with
the detached observer's eye. Never for one moment had I
really reconciled myself to losing Barry; never had I really
forgiven him for not being what I wanted him to be. All those
years of manic creative activity had served only to postpone
the inevitable breakdown. Something had to set it off some
day, and it happened to be Brent's physical resemblance to
Barry. I was not the least bit interested in Brent as a person;
I was interested only in recreating my image of Barry.

Once this had become clear I was able to think back without pain. It was as if all the bitterness and resentment that
had been suppressed during those fifteen years of trying to
blot out my life with Barry had flared up and burst forth and
now, with the poison at last drained away, that wound had a
chance to heal.

But I was very exhausted. It was an effort to string a few
words together, let alone act my Helen Mitchell self. After
nearly falling asleep over lunch with an English couple whom
I knew slightly and who happened to be holidaying in the
same neighborhood, I suggested to Brent that we should either postpone or cut out altogether some of the visits we had
proposed to make. He was very annoyed. What was the point
of his coming as chauffeur, he wanted to know, if we weren't
going to go anywhere? Besides, he wanted to go to the big
places and meet people in the literary scene. If he'd known I
was going to stick here up in the mountains all the time he
would never have come. He wanted to show himself off as a
modern English novelist, make the right contacts, get on to
the circuit. He had understood that this was one of the main
reasons for the journey.

"It was," I said wearily, "and still is. You won't miss
anything, I promise you. But I've got to have some rest first."

He continued to sulk and I continued to soothe for some
time. Eventually he came and knelt by my chair and buried
his head in my lap and said:

"I'm very mean to you. I'm sorry, Helen. It's because I'm
not happy either."

This was just the sort of situation that I had revelled in
during the weeks of my madness and it was not his fault that
I was now coming through to a clearer vision. I had in fact

been "using" him, as he himself had guessed. But it had been to work out my own situation, not to experiment with his feelings. For a moment I thought of telling him this; he deserved an explanation for my extraordinary behaviour and it would do us both good to get on to a more honest footing. But the impulse was soon quashed. It would be too cruel to tell him that he as a unique human creature was of no consequence to me whatever; better let him go on believing that I was observing his reactions, for to be the subject of scientific enquiry could not, in our science-ridden age, be thought incompatible with human dignity.

I stroked his hair and let him talk. The usual confused, aggressive apologies. The only thing that came across clearly and honestly was that he really was unhappy. There was a very deep-rooted self-hatred and frustration and insecurity—the sort of thing one sees in young delinquents. What he needed was a good, simple and utterly reliable mother substitute who would make him feel loved and wanted at all times and with whom he need never pretend. Playing lovers with a middle-aged woman who was only interested in her own emotions was no good to him at all, particularly when she was a writer to whom he had to play second fiddle all the time.

I sought for something to say that would show my genuine concern.

"Is the book not going well, Brent?" I asked.

It was a sign of how little I regarded him that I had almost forgotten the plan for his novel.

"It's all right," he snapped. "You know I don't want to talk about it."

"I'm sorry," I said in sincere remorse. How horribly patronizing and complacent I must sound to him! An ever-present reminder of his own lack of inspiration. And I did not even provide a primitive boost to his male ego, as no doubt his little dark and secretive Jean did, since my boredom with our love-making was too strong to be hidden.

However, there we both were, dumped into this false position by my own doing and it was up to me to get us out of it. I found myself obliged to study Brent not as a means of gratification but as a person in his own right. I didn't like him at all as a person, but a feeling of guilt and a sense of justice drove me to try to treat him fairly.

It was my own fault. I had craved for a close personal involvement and now I had got it, though not in the form I should have chosen. If only, when I felt myself so cut off from other people, I had opened up to them more gradually and more wisely. I could have tried to enter into Philip's interests with sympathy instead of barely concealed sarcasm. Even Dora would surely have responded to a little genuine goodwill from my side. Or I could have been more forbearing towards Marian, and taken up our old relationship again once the heat generated by the moment of truth had subsided. Forty years of friendship ought not to be so lightly thrown away. And Mrs. Simmonds, longing to be protective. She might well have been indulged a little without an intolerable invasion of my privacy.

Thus my thoughts ran on while I went through a routine of love-making with Brent. A new image of Helen Mitchell was emerging—no longer cynical, but wise, tolerant, and genuinely charitable towards others. And the novels would be very different from those that had gone before—the sort of stuff that sometimes emerges from a big personal crisis in a writer's life. Not so popular perhaps. But artistically superior? I could but do my best. The itch to begin was stirring already. And I saw Helen Mitchell herself in a little cottage, compact and tidy, with a cat and an old-fashioned garden, in the heart of a village. She would be active in local affairs, knowing everybody, and with a door always open to anyone who wanted to come in. Just like a village postmistress, or like Mr. Evans the newsagent back home.

But at the recollection of Mr. Evans, that harmless and obliging little postmaster, my charming fantasy came to an end and was succeeded by a very unpleasant train of thought.

"Brent," I said, "did any mail forwarded from England arrive today?"

"Not that I've seen," he replied in some surprise. We had been talking in a desultory manner about the people in the hotel and this was an abrupt change of subject.

"Then there's been nothing for three days."

"It must be held up in the post. It can't be Jean's fault. She said she'd send it on every day."

He spoke with a mixture of embarrassment and defensiveness, as he always did when referring to Jean.

"You don't think it's because she's annoyed at our coming away together?" I asked.

"Of course not," he snapped.

But I was far from reassured. Most heartily did I wish, now in my return to sanity, that I had not left Jean Graves with the free run of my house. As Mrs. Simmonds had sensibly pointed out, I knew nothing about her except what Brent had told me. She was employed by one of the big hotels, which might be some guarantee of her honesty, but I was not so much worried that she would run off with valuables—which would be foolish because it could be proved against her—as that she would snoop around my possessions. The thought of those pale, cold fingers opening my cupboards, turning over my clothes, trying on coats, shoes, dresses, perhaps even "borrowing" them, made me shudder. Of course Mrs. Simmonds had been in my house for a day or two after my departure and Mr. Thorburn had a key . . . nevertheless, for very many hours Jean would be able to do what she liked and it was too much to hope that she would have no curiosity at all. The most chilling thought of all was that she might take it into her head to look at the papers on and in my desk, and it was made infinitely worse by the horrible suspicion that had just come to me.

It was like those occasions when, many miles from home, one suddenly remembers that a saucepan has been left burning on the gas. But in this case there was no simple solution like ringing up a friendly neighbour and begging him to investigate. I could not tell anybody that I had been so crazy as not to know whether or not I had actually dispatched an important parcel, still less could I reveal why the contents were so vital.

Those diaries that I ought to have destroyed many years ago, holding the secrets not only of my own life but of Barry's. And what secrets! Lord Walters, the nation's preserver—revealed as a cheat, as corrupt as they make them. What a find for any unscrupulous person who knew how to interpret the diary's contents. If the notebooks were to fall into the wrong hands . . .

I was burning as with fever and at the same time I was

shot through and through with icy shafts. It can't have happened, I told myself firmly; it's a common psychological phenomenon, this mix-up of fears and suppressed wishes; you're only frightened that you could be the means of ruining Barry just because something in you wants so much to have revenge on him. You haven't done it; those explosive documents are safe in a sealed package at the bank.

"You've heard from Jean, haven't you?" I said to Brent. "Does she say anything about how things are at home?"

He fished a letter out of a pocket and glanced through it.

"Oh yes," he said. "I forgot to tell you. One of the plants seems to be dying. She's afraid she may have given it too much water."

"Damn the plants!" I exclaimed. "It's letters I'm worrying about. I ought to have heard from the bank by now acknowledging the parcel I sent off just before we came away, but nothing has come from them."

"Parcel?" echoed Brent. "What parcel?"

"The one I left with Mr. Evans at the post office."

"But it was Sunday morning. The post office wasn't open."

"I know, I know," I cried impatiently. "Mr. Evans was going to dispatch it for me next day."

Brent was frowning. "I don't remember your going to the post office," he said.

"Don't you?" I replied feebly, searching my memory for reassurance.

What had happened during those last hectic days? The overwhelming need to get away after I had learnt that Mrs. Simmonds was to work for Barry. The nightmarish farewell party; the terrible hours of darkness that had followed, and the lucid interval when I had realized that I must remove my diaries and my typescripts to a safe place. That was clear enough. I had decided upon a sensible course of action. But had I ever carried it out?

"It's very kind of you, Mr. Evans," I could hear myself saying, "they're urgent proofs. I ought to have sent them back before."

And he had replied . . . what had he replied? Chubby and cheerful Mr. Evans. He must have said something. Had he wished me bon voyage? Had he asked when the next book was coming out? Had he been surprised that I was setting off a day earlier than planned?

The more I tried to concentrate on remembering, the blanker my mind became.

Brent was looking at me curiously.

"Oh, don't you remember?" I said as casually as I could. "I slipped along to the post office while you were loading the car. I hope Mr. Evans didn't let me down."

"What was in the parcel?" asked Brent, and then a moment later, before I had time to think up a reply, he added petulantly: "You ought to have asked me to do it. I don't know why you're paying me to be your secretary if it's not to relieve you of chores like that. Of course if you don't trust me—"

"My dear, you had more than enough to do already. And actually it wasn't all that important—only some share certificates and a few other documents that I'd been meaning to send off for some time."

It sounded very unconvincing, but to my great relief he said no more about it beyond remarking that banks were so inefficient nowadays that I would probably never get an acknowledgement at all. This remark comforted me. It might well be true; or perhaps their acknowledgement had been wrongly addressed or wrongly delivered; or it might be in an envelope that looked like a circular and Jean had slipped it in among the periodicals and other packets that she had been asked to pile up on the table in the drawing-room. As I thought of all the possible reasons why I had heard nothing from the bank I gradually grew calmer in mind, and after a while was even able to catch a glimpse of the happier future that had been filling my thoughts before the appalling suspicion had blotted out everything else. Besides, even if the worst had happened, and I had in fact left those documents in the drawer of my desk, there was no certainty that Jean would find the key or that the papers would mean anything to her if she did discover them.

Brent might have told her about the unpublished novels, but he knew nothing about the diaries. They were closely written, often with no dates inserted and with one entry running straight on into another. It would be difficult to decipher the handwriting, and someone unversed in such matters might well take them for the rough draft of a novel.

For a long time I laboured over my excuses and explana-

tions in my mind, polishing them up and improving on them,
making them word perfect. I was no longer trying to convince
a suspicious and possibly vindictive Jean Graves; I was trying
to make them credible to the reader of a novel. The habit of
creating fiction was very very strong, and my mental breakdown had not destroyed it.

Gradually the anxiety died away to a steady nagging. I
could, of course, have learned the truth about the parcel by
telephoning either the bank or the postmaster, but I could not
bring myself to do this. There was a strong desire to hold on
to all the alternative explanations for as long as possible, and
besides, I was finding it difficult to make any decisions at all.
Coping with Brent was as much as I could manage. His nervous tantrums were becoming more and more frequent, but
he was determined to extract the very last dregs from our tour
and I dared not suggest that we should cut it short and go
home. Seeing him now as himself and not as a nostalgic echo
of Barry, I found that in addition to feeling ill at ease with
him I was also becoming apprehensive. There was a strain of
viciousness in him that I had been blind to before; he was
capable of turning nasty if he felt he was being patronized or
his self-esteem being threatened. And this, of course, was
constantly happening since at all the gatherings we attended
it was I who was the leading figure.

We left the little resort up in the pine forests and visited
Munich and Stuttgart, Mannheim and Heidelberg, Frankfurt
and Cologne, staying a couple of days in each city and driving
the hundreds of miles of autobahn at a terrifying speed. When
I ventured to suggest slowing down he reminded me that I
had once told him I didn't care how fast he drove. Out of
sheer self-protection I had to be constantly soothing his ego.
He was burned up with envy of my books and my reputation,
and I was totally powerless to bring him ease. It might have
helped a little if I had been able to convince him that I was
madly in love with him: the writer might have been forgiven
if the woman had sufficiently flattered his vanity. I tried my
best but it was a pitiful attempt.

In the end, the strain and the travelling and the ever-nagging
worry about the whereabouts of my precious documents
brought me to such a pitch of exhaustion that for a few days
I was physically ill. Brent made a little show of being con-

siderate then, but by the time we were back on the Channel ferry once more we had nearly reached the point of hating each other, and I was planning how we could part company for ever without first going through the miseries of quarrels and reproaches and all the rest of it.

But by that time I had lost the illusion that I was in control of events. Another mind had taken over the plot and was directing the action, and I could do no more than struggle to defend myself. I was caught fast in a trap—a trap of my own making. It would need every bit of ingenuity and imagination that I possessed to extricate myself from it and there was no guarantee of success. It might already be too late.

PART TWO

11

"I've been thinking, Brent," I said as we drove away from Dover, "that I might find someone else to come and type for me. You ought to be getting on with your own book now, and I am planning a heavy round of activity for myself."

"Well as a matter of fact," he began, and then he swore as we had to swerve out of the thunderous path of a monster lorry.

When conversation was once more possible I asked how it was going. I knew this was going to annoy him, but I really did need to know.

"There's not been much time to write lately, has there?" he said. "However, it's going all right."

He was lying. I had come to know him so well that I could recognize the slight jerk of the head and the increased tempo of speech that showed he was concealing his thoughts. The novel was not progressing well.

I stared ahead and did not speak again for some time.

The Kent countryside looked small and neat and welcoming. I was desperately impatient to be home and yet at the same time I was dreading the arrival. Again and again I told myself that my documents were either at the bank or else lying safely in the drawer. Any other supposition was simply a paranoiac fantasy resulting from the state of near mental breakdown from which I had so miraculously recovered. I would get rid of Brent, sell the house, and start on my new lease of life—a new cycle of creation.

"What about the car?" asked Brent suddenly.

"What about it? It's running all right, isn't it?"

"Yes, of course. I meant will you be keeping it? If you don't want me to go on working for you, I mean."

He braked violently and thumped on the horn as a mini shot out of a side road without warning.

"It's not my car," I said. "It's yours."

"But I can't accept it if I'm not going to—oh hell."

Again he had to stand on the brakes. We weren't far from home so there was no reason why I should endure his nerve-racking driving any longer.

"I don't know why you are in such a temper," I said mildly, "but I think it might be best if you drop me at the station when we get to Hastings and I'll finish the journey by train."

He sulked after that, but at least our progress was less terrifying.

"D'you want us to clear out of the flat too?" he said after a while.

"Not unless you want to move. You've got a lease. You're paying the rent."

We were on a comparatively quiet stretch of road now, with wide grass verges. Suddenly we bumped up on to the grass and came to a screeching, bone-shaking halt.

"What's the matter?" I asked. "Tyre gone?"

"I've got to get this straight," he said, grimacing at the steering-wheel and wrenching it violently around: "Are you trying to tell me I've got the sack? Because if so I'd like to know why. I don't know what you expect in the way of a secretary/chauffeur, but as far as I can see I've done all that is required and a hell of a lot more, and given up a lot of extra time, and I certainly never asked for any expensive presents, and if you mean to leave me high and dry now without a salary and with an expensive flat to run and a half-finished book after practically forcing me to give up my other flat and to start on this experiment as you call it, then I think it's—I think it's—well, it isn't what I'd expected of you."

I let him rave on. The sun was very glaring and I held up a hand to shade my eyes. Perhaps he thought he had reduced me to tears, because he stopped tearing at the steering-wheel and twisted round towards me and said with an assumption

of feeling that would have been ludicrous if it had not been
so embarrassing:

"I'm sorry, Helen. It's not that I'm not grateful. You know
how much it means to me—how much *you* mean to me."

"There's no question of my giving you the sack," I said.
"I was only concerned that you might be neglecting your own
work, but if you feel you can manage it, then of course we
will carry on with the present arrangement for the time being."

Insincerity is catching and perpetuates itself; my own tones
seemed to me to be drenched in it, and Brent's reaction was
terrible. It looked as if getting rid of him kindly and tactfully
was going to be out of the question and drastic measures
would have to be taken. But now was not the moment. When
I was safely home and within call of other people, and above
all, when I was reassured as to the safety of my precious
diaries, then I would have the strength to resist emotional
blackmail and throw off this parasite that I had so lovingly
entwined about myself.

Jean came up the area steps as we drew up at the house and
handed me the front door key.

I greeted her with a blazingly artificial smile and I saw a
look pass between her and Brent before they exchanged any
words. It seemed to me that she gave a barely perceptible
nod. Reassuring him? Giving him the go-ahead? Or had I
imagined it?

Mr. Thorburn then appeared and told me how glad he was
to see me home. Brent was at that moment extracting luggage
from the back of the car and Mr. Thorburn acknowledged his
greeting with a curt nod. Jean he ignored completely, and
when my conversation with her was concluded he made a
little show to indicate that he wanted to speak to me privately.

"Come in for a drink this evening," I said, "and let me
bore you with my traveller's tales."

Then Brent carried up my cases and Jean followed him
with some of the smaller pieces, like the chambermaid waiting on the head porter, so that I felt as if my own house was
a hotel. It turned out that she wanted to apologize for the
dead geraniums on the balcony and to make me some tea.
There was a mute persistence about the girl that was as dif-

ficult to counter as Brent's more obvious tactics, and the
quickest way to get rid of them all seemed to be to accept
the offer.

So I sat on the settee and was brought a tray, though actually I was much more restless and anxious than tired, and
would have liked to potter around in my own kitchen. Mrs.
Simmonds would have allowed me to, I thought, and I was
suddenly assailed with a great sense of loss. My nice, pink,
honest and bustling Mrs. Simmonds, whose presence I had
grown used to and who had got used to my ways—I had sent
her away in my temporary madness and there was no chance
of getting her back. Barry and his lady—Rita Rendall that
was—would make quite sure of that.

Jean was holding out a few letters.

"These came today," she murmured.

Brent snatched them from her.

"She doesn't want them now," he snapped.

The voice he used to Jean, I noted, was very different from
that in which he spoke to me.

"Just leave them on the table," I said as pleasantly as I
could, "along with the parcels. I'll look at the mail when
I've had tea."

They made me feel sickened and ashamed between them.
It was like a scene from a hackneyed thriller; unscrupulous
young couple sponging on rich older woman. But I was no
longer a willing participant in this drama that I myself had
set in motion; there was no longer the slightest confusion in
my mind between fiction and fact. This was my life and it
was disgusting. I should be very lucky indeed if it didn't
become even worse.

At last they could find no further excuse for staying and
they went downstairs. In a flash I was at the roll-top desk. The
long drawer was locked. I opened the little drawer above the
pigeon-holes and saw the key lying innocently among pins
and paperclips and other odds and ends. I inserted it in the
lock of the long drawer and pulled it open; it was empty—no
diaries, no typescripts, no papers whatsoever. So I did pack
up that parcel and send it off, I muttered to myself.

I put my mind into blinkers; I would not admit any other
possibility. And yet it was with shaking fingers that I turned

over the letters that had arrived at the house since the last forwarding of mail. There was nothing from the bank.

I went to the telephone in a sort of frozen calm and dialled the number; they were not yet closed and the clerk with whom I normally dealt was still there. I explained that I had asked somebody to send off some documents for me and had reason to suppose that they had never been posted.

While he went away to investigate I stared out of the window. It was a bright and gusty October day. Great white clouds raced across the sky, white waves leapt up to meet them. I described them in my mind, polishing up the phrases. Anything to stop myself thinking.

At last the clerk came back to the phone. "The last time we heard from you," he said, "with a request for safekeeping was about eighteen months ago. Some share certificates. I can give you the details if you like. Would that be it?"

"Oh no. It's much more recent than that."

I refused to believe it and yet I had to believe it. This was no novel; this was really happening.

"We always acknowledge receipt the same day," said the clerk with faint reproach.

I forced myself to be bright and breezy.

"Oh I know. I didn't really think there was much hope and I'm sorry to have troubled you—but when it's a question of searching through huge cupboards full of junk . . ."

After ringing off I sat still for a few minutes taking deep breaths. Then I got up and opened one of the long windows and peered over the balcony to make sure that neither Brent nor Jean was hanging about the area steps and that I could leave the house unseen.

I ran to the newsagent's shop and bought an evening paper.

"And perhaps you will start regular deliveries again to-morrow," I said. "You've got the list, haven't you, Mr. Evans?"

"It shall be done."

That was the moment for him to mention the parcel if by some miracle I had handed it to him and it had failed to reach its destination. The post office section was now closed, but I hovered around the stationery counter.

"Can I interest you in our new line?" said Mr. Evans, holding up a piece of board cut in the shape of an elephant, with little memo pads attached to the tusks. "You're meant to hang this up in the kitchen and note your shopping needs on it. Isn't it horrible? But people buy them, they do."

I laughed. "An aide memoire. That's just what I need! I've taken to forgetting which letters I have written and which I haven't. And which parcels I have sent off. I didn't send a big package via your office just before I went away by any chance, did I?"

"Not that I remember. Lost some proofs, have you? That's a pity. Perhaps you handed them to Winnie."

He called across the shop to Mrs. Evans. No, she couldn't recall anything. She was sure she would remember if I had sent such a parcel.

And so the last little flicker of hope was extinguished.

I walked slowly back to the house, face to face with the inescapable truth. Somebody, during my absence, had found the key to the long drawer of the desk, and had removed the diaries, the typescripts, and the letters and cuttings. This was theft, and had it been money or jewelry I would have called the police right away and put up with all the consequent domestic unpleasantness and possible newspaper publicity. But at the thought of explaining the present situation to the police and having it all made public my courage fell. It would make a good story—the *Case of the Missing Manuscripts*—but would it ensure that they were returned to me? If Jean had taken them she would be prepared for a search and she would have made quite sure they would not be found in the basement flat. And who else was there? Mrs. Simmonds? Mr. Thorburn? The notion was absurd. Such unpromising suspects would do in fiction but not in life.

It must be Jean. On Brent's instructions. They had planned it together. Motive? The unpublished novels, of course; the diaries and letters had been thrown in as a bonus. And what were they proposing to do? Demand a ransom for returning my kidnapped brain-child? Or get rid of me and produce the novels as Brent's own work? That was it, of course. That would account for all his jumpiness and his tantrums, his alternate bullying and conciliatory attitude towards me. It was his story now; his imagination was spinning the plot. It was a bolder scheme than I would ever have given him credit for—but had he the nerve to carry it through?

I sat down at my desk when I got back to the drawing-room and forced myself to take a cool look at this theory. Brent was desperate for another big dose of fame as a writer and he would stick at nothing to achieve it. That was a matter of fact, not fiction. The little burst of genuine creativity that had resulted from my taking him under my wing had quickly fizzled out and left him more hopeless than ever. My own idiotic behaviour had planted this seed of an idea in his mind and with Jean as accomplice he had successfully carried through the first stage of the plot. The next stage would be to lie low for a time and be prepared for blank denial should I decide to call in the police. Meanwhile he would be making changes in my manuscripts, putting his own characteristic touches upon them. He was writer enough to make a passable job of it. And instead of the new model Helen Mitchell there would be a new model Brent Ashwood—author of only two books, admittedly, making three publications in all, but many a writer's reputation had rested upon even less.

Thus far had I got in my speculations when the front door bell rang. I started violently; my nerves were very much out of control. But it was only Mr. Thorburn, whom I had temporarily forgotten. Perhaps I could learn something from him; it was worth a try.

I poured him a drink and said:

"Do I gather that you had something to tell me?"

"Yes indeed." He watched me, frowning, his small thin mouth, drooping at the corners.

"Well, go ahead."

I handed him his glass and raised my own.

"To your good health. And to the next Helen Mitchell—provided I can find it! It's practically ready for publication but at the moment I seem to have mislaid the fair copy."

I watched him keenly as I spoke. It was inconceivable that he could have stolen my manuscripts. But the diaries? Was it quite out of the question that he had snooped around and come across them and realized their significance? I knew nothing about him except that he had been an accountant in the City. He might quite well have at one time had some connection with Barry.

"Really?" said Mr. Thorburn in a disbelieving tone of

voice. "I trust it will soon turn up. You take carbons, I presume?"

"Oh yes."

We sipped at our drinks in silence.

"Miss Mitchell," he said presently, "I have something rather difficult for me to say, since it is very foreign to my nature to question the judgment of a lady in your position for whom I have a very lively respect and regard."

He stopped abruptly. It's about the only lively thing about you, I said to myself.

"However," he continued, "I am sure you will appreciate that my motives are good and that you will understand that I have been accustomed throughout my working years to offer advice to a number of people whose talents lie in the artistic rather than in the business field."

"I quite understand," I replied, stopping myself just in time from saying tartly that he was wasting his breath because I already had an accountant. The tiresome man would have to be allowed to come to the point in his own way.

It was a long, meandering and wearisome way, but had it been a jet flight it would have spelled out the words: Don't trust Jean Graves.

"I hope you aren't saying this just because she and Brent aren't married," I said.

"Oh no, no."

He was terribly shocked at the suggestion that he was so easily shockable.

"Oh no, indeed. I hope I realize that one must move with the times in this respect, but to abuse somebody's trust is quite another matter."

After several more diversions I got out of him at last that on two occasions Jean had invited a few people in and had taken glasses and cutlery and other items from my cupboards.

"Is that all!" I cried. "I said she could borrow things if she liked. I hope they didn't go on all night and keep you awake?"

I was very disappointed. All I had gained from my lengthy endurance test was the information that Mr. Thorburn, taking it upon himself to count the spoons, had challenged Jean with taking things down to her flat and she had been very abusive. This last I found difficult to envisage, even allowing for the fact that so many of the rude words are monosyllables.

"I suppose you didn't see her removing any books or papers," I said. "That's what's worrying me at the moment."

Apart from expressing a belief that she was capable of anything, he did not react to this remark. Either he was exactly what he seemed—too stupid to imagine that someone might have an interest in other things than silver; or else he was very cleverly suggesting to me that Jean had stolen the papers, but without giving away that he even knew of their existence.

There was, however, a surprise to come.

"Naturally I didn't mention a word of this to your brother," Mr. Thorburn said.

"To my brother!" I exclaimed. "Nobody told me Phil had been here."

Apparently the visit had taken place about a week previously, when Jean was out at work. Mr. Thorburn had come in on one of the spoon-checking forays—I forebore to comment that there seemed to have been an excessive number of them—and had answered the bell to Philip, who "happened to be down in Brighton visiting a colleague about a case on which he was engaged."

"I trust you both refreshed yourselves," I said, waving my hand at the tray of drinks.

But Mr. Thorburn was impervious to irony. "Thank you, yes, we did," he said soberly. "And we also had a most interesting and enjoyable conversation before I departed, leaving him here to rest for a while. I understood that he would be getting in touch with you."

"No doubt he will, and the mystery will then be solved."

I could scarcely keep the excitement out of my voice. A wild hope had entered in. Phil had been alone in this room; Phil knew the ways of our father's old desk and it always had fascinated him. He'd been looking it over, of course; opened up all the drawers, found what he would instantly recognize to be very private papers left easily accessible to all and sundry, sworn at my imbecile carelessness, and taken them off for safe keeping. I would phone him as soon as Mr. Thorburn had gone; or perhaps he would ring me.

I wanted to dance with relief, to cry aloud "Thank God, thank God." If Phil had got the documents all would be well. Even Dora, detestable woman though she was, would be discreet over a matter like this. Family honour meant a lot to her. Mr. Thorburn departed at last and almost immediately afterwards the phone rang. I leapt to it: let it be Phil, I prayed; let this nightmare be over.

It was a wrong number. And then there was a call from a local journalist; and then my agents, and then Marian—subdued and conciliatory and obviously wanting to be friends again. And then at last, when my mind was exhausted with the effort of talking briefly about my holiday, and my heart sick with hope deferred, came the call from my brother.

"I've been trying to get you for ages," he said testily.

"I know, dear. I'm sorry. I've not been back for long and everyone is phoning at once."

Hurry up, I muttered under my breath, don't do a Mr. Thorburn on me.

"I can't hear you," said Phil even more irritably. "This is a very bad line."

"I'm sorry I missed you," I said loudly, "when you came down last week. I gather my neighbour let you in."

"Yes. He seemed to be making himself very much at home. However, it's your house, not mine."

"What do you mean?" I cried, no longer trying to hide my impatience. "What was he doing?"

"Well, he had no difficulty in finding the whiskey and I should think he'd been helping himself to it pretty liberally before I came."

Mr. Thorburn—a secret drinker? At the moment this was completely irrelevant.

"Damn the whiskey!" I exploded. "It's not *that* that's worrying me. It's my papers. You didn't get the feeling that he'd been looking at things in my desk, did you?"

"Why? Is something missing?"

"I don't know yet. I've not had time to check. But it did seem that somebody might have been going through the drawers of the desk."

Now was the moment for him to speak. Past the moment, in fact. Even if Phil thought I had been wickedly careless and needed teaching a lesson, he would surely never have drawn out the agony like this.

"Don't you keep everything of importance locked up?" was all he said.

"Oh yes. But I still don't like to think that people have been snooping around. Let's forget it."

If he had been in the room I would have told him everything, but telephone conversations are not the same. We exchanged a few items of news and then he reverted to the subject of his own accord:

"What about that new secretary of yours—can you trust him?"

"Brent? He came away with me. He was driving."

"His girl-friend, then?"

"Oh, she's a simple little thing. She wouldn't be interested in books and papers."

What a stupid thing to say when in fact I was longing to share my fears with Philip!

"Well I suppose you know best," he said grudgingly. "What exactly is it that's missing? You've not gone and left your will lying around, I hope."

This last came as an anxious afterthought. Trust Philip to think of my will.

"My will," I said coldly, "is lodged with a local solicitor, as you know. If you would prefer to have it in your office I will arrange for it to be sent to you. You are sole executor, as you also know, and you will also remember that apart from some legacies to charities and one or two people to whom I owe a debt of gratitude, you inherit everything. It will be a substantial sum. Of course royalties will continue to accumulate after my decease. I have no intention of making any alteration. Perhaps you will be good enough to convey this information to Dora and set her mind at rest."

Philip protested that he had not been thinking about it at all and indeed I regretted my harshness even as I spoke. It was a poor look-out for my good resolution of getting on to better terms with the family.

I apologized. "Look, Phil," I added, "I really am worried to death but I can't tell you on the phone. Will you be coming this way again soon?"

He hummed and hawed and said he would try to make it next week, adding half-heartedly that of course I could always come up to town and see him in the office if I preferred to. I said I would think about it and rang off, feeling dampened and deflated as I so often was after a conversation with Philip.

—————— 12 ——————

The following morning I decided that I could no longer postpone the evil hour when I had to speak to Brent and Jean. I got rid of Brent by asking him to take the car to the garage for servicing. He was in an ingratiating mood and made no protest. Then I approached Jean with the greatest circumspection, laying all the blame on my own carelessness and forgetfulness.

As expected, there was not the faintest sign of emotion on that deadpan face, not even righteous indignation. She could not remember ever having gone near the desk—she had piled up the circulars and parcels on the table, as instructed. No, she had seen nothing of the sort of papers I described.

Had anyone else been upstairs? What about the people she had invited in? No, they had none of them come upstairs. There had only been three of them—two waiters and a chambermaid from the hotel, but she had borrowed some of my things because she wanted to make a nice party of it and because I had said she might do so.

She said all this in a small, respectful voice, her hands held lightly together in front of her. Apart from the discovery that she was capable of saying more than "yes" and "no," I gained nothing from the interview. Even when I tempted her to accuse Mr. Thorburn she was very careful to say nothing specific, and at no point did she show any sign of taking my enquiries as an accusation against herself, nor did she show any interest at all in the missing documents. In fact

she was so cleverly unrevealing that I could not help thinking
that she must have had experience in parrying police enquiries. She had just the nerves and the temperament to be a
successful little thief and it had certainly taken more than her
straight earnings to keep herself and Brent in an expensive
flat. The moment she had gone I rang her hotel manager,
which of course I should have done before, and asked for a
reference for her as a prospective tenant. The answer was, of
course, that she was discreet, efficient and reliable and had
excellent references from previous employers.

Apart from this, the only outcome of my talk with Jean
was a renewed suspicion that I myself was responsible for the
misplacing of the documents. If my mental confusion had
been such that I did not know whether or not I had posted a
parcel, then I could equally well have hidden the papers away
and forgotten about it. I persuaded myself that before speaking to Brent it would be wise to search my whole house.
Marian happened to ring at that moment and I told her some
part of the story and enlisted her help, admitting that I had
behaved very foolishly and giving her every opportunity to
wallow in the magnanimity of not saying "I told you so."

"We'll have to go through everything," she said briskly.
"It'll take a couple of days at least. I'd better stay with you
overnight—I've not got much on this week."

To examine every possible place of concealment on the
three floors above ground level was indeed a formidable task.
Every cupboard was turned out, every book removed from
the shelves, the contents of every drawer sifted.

"Surely I couldn't have climbed up there!" I cried as Marian dragged a stepladder over to the trapdoor and flashed her
torch around the little loft where the storage tank was in-
stalled.

"We'd better look everywhere," she said, "while we're
about it. You've got such a wild imagination, my dear Nell,
that I wouldn't put anything past you."

I thanked her humbly. I was grateful to her for keeping up
the pretence that it was I myself who had hidden away the
documents, for I had no doubt that she had other suspicions
in mind. Brent's face alone, when he opened the drawing-
room door and found Marian and me breakfasting together,
was an eloquent giveaway.

She looked at him in surprise. "Mr. Ashwood? I believe we have met." And then, turning to me: "I didn't hear the front doorbell. Did you, Nell?"

Feebly I started to defend Brent for walking in. He had a key . . . I liked to know someone was able to get in and check that all was well . . . when one lived alone . . . and so on.

Brent was freezingly polite to Marian but he gave me a look that said plainly: you are going to suffer for this later.

"Miss Gray is helping me spring clean," I said. "It was never done earlier this year for some reason or other, and since she so kindly offered . . . I don't suppose you want to come and wield a duster, do you? I thought perhaps you might like a couple of days off duty after all the driving you've been doing for me."

I was very conscious that Marian was summing up the situation between Brent and myself and most relieved when he took himself off with a shrug, saying: "Oh well, if you really don't want me for a day or two . . ."

All that day we continued our search. When at last we decided to stop there was not a single square inch that had not been gone over and I was the gainer by a beautifully clean and tidy home and a few small household items that had been missing for some time.

"Well, that's that," said Marian as we slumped exhausted on to the settee. "If you did hide them it was done so well that they'll never come to light again. It rather looks as if you're going to have to sit down and write those books all over again. Unless . . ."

Her voice trailed away. I knew only too well what was coming; it could not be postponed any longer.

"Unless they are in the basement flat," she said tactfully. "Would you like me to help you look there? At a convenient time, of course."

In other words, when Brent and Jean were out. I had kept a key to the flat and I considered the suggestion. If they were indeed guilty, then they would know perfectly well what Marian and I were looking for, and they would expect us to search the basement at the first opportunity. Nothing would be found there. The thought of going through other people's personal possessions was very repulsive to me. Besides, it would take a little time, and it would be exceedingly unpleasant to be caught in the act. That would precipitate the showdown that clearly had to come and that I was so greatly dreading. Better perhaps choose my own moment for talking to Brent and leave the search of the basement till later.

I said as much to Marian.

She raised her eyebrows.

"You can guess what I really think, Nell, but I didn't want to upset you. Would you like me to tackle him about it?"

It was an idea. He seemed to be scared of Marian, so totally impervious to his charm had she proved herself. On the other hand she did not know him as I did and she would not be able to recognize the little signs that might give him away. And I could also do a bit of bluffing that might well provoke a reaction or at any rate throw a spanner in the works of his plot. So I thanked Marian and promised to phone her as soon as I had talked to Brent.

At nine o'clock the next morning he knocked on the drawing-room door and peered round it with an affectation of diffidence.

"Is the she-dragon gone?"

"We've finished the cleaning," I said briskly, "and there's a lot of mail to deal with. We'd better clear off the accumulation first."

We worked for a couple of hours, during which time Brent was exaggeratedly polite, scarcely speaking except to say such things as "Yes, ma'am," "Certainly, ma'am," and "you're the boss" with an assumed American accent that got on my nerves more and more every minute. By mid-day I was wishing I had let Marian handle it after all; she could not have made more of a hash of it than I was going to.

"Let's stop," I cried suddenly in the middle of dictating a letter of thanks to one of our German hosts. "I'm sick of all this pretending. Get me a drink."

I watched him swagger over with the brimming glasses. He handed me mine and raised his own:

"To the next Helen Mitchell."

It seemed to me that there was a sneer in his voice.

"Thank you," I replied as calmly as I could. "I would drink to it gladly if only I knew where it was at this moment."

"Knew where it was?" he echoed, registering surprise, puzzlement, and a dawning understanding. "Have you lost the manuscript? Is *that* what you've been looking for in your marathon spring-clean?"

"Yes," I said regarding him closely.

He gulped down his drink and began to laugh—a horrid sound.

"That's great, that sure is. Tidy to the point of obsession and then goes and loses her own manuscript—her own infant best-seller."

"You're drunk, Brent," I said sharply.

"On two whiskies? You've got to be joking."

He gave me a slobbering kiss and then went to pour out another drink. I felt physically sick, both with disgust and apprehension. I was not going to be able to cope; I ought to have let Marian deal with this. I stood up and gripped the back of the settee.

"Have you got my typescripts, Brent?" I asked. "The two novels I told you about, that were in the drawer of the desk. They're not there now, and I can't find them anywhere in the house."

He laughed again. "You sent them away. To the bank. Don't you remember?"

Once more he came over and kissed me. "Never mind, old girl. It's a sure sign of genius, they say. Absent-mindedness."

He flung himself into a chair and looked like staying there, much to my relief. Provided he kept at a distance I might be able to salvage something from this unpromising beginning.

"I am afraid I took the thought for the deed," I said, "as sometimes happens when one is very tired and preoccupied. I have checked up all round and there is no doubt that I never sent off that parcel. So that when we went away the two type-scripts were in the drawer. When we got back they were gone."

Should I mention the diaries? No, better not. There was still a faint chance that he had not grasped their full significance.

"And I'm supposed to have removed them, have I?" he said. "On a flying foray from Frankfurt while you were being fêted at the Fair? What a lot of effs. Language, language. Steady now, Brent. The lady doesn't like it.''

"Not you, of course," I said, "but Jean was here."

"Jean!" He exploded into laughter. "Poor little Jean. She doesn't know one end of a book from the other."

I hesitated what to say next. Every word he uttered, every gesture he made was convincing me of his guilt. But it would have been so much simpler if I could have accused him of taking the books himself rather than of giving instructions to Jean to do so. It would place me in a hopelessly difficult position if he chose to wax indignant on her behalf, but this, of course, was just what he proceeded to do.

"Now look here, Helen." He leaned forward in his chair. Instinctively I took a step nearer the door; if he touched me again I was going to vomit. "Now see here—I won't have you accusing Jean of rifling your desk when you left her in charge of the house. If you didn't think she was trustworthy then you bloody well oughtn't to have left her with the key. If you were just trying to catch her out, well, there's names for people who do that sort of thing, not very nice ones. I quite understand that you're jealous of Jean and you'd like me to give her up and concentrate on you. Well I'm not going to. I told you so from the start. You've done a hell of a lot for me, but so has she. Besides, I need her. You're not bad for your age, I admit, but she's really good in bed, as those quiet ones often are. I'm sorry, Helen. I know just how you must feel. It's bloody awful, being jealous. But to try to get rid of Jean by framing her, sticking a theft on her—well, I'm disappointed. I just didn't think you would do a thing like that, that's all.''

I heard him out to the end, speechless and astounded. Not so much at the line he was taking as at my own stupidity for not realizing at the outset that he was going to take this line. Self-centered fool that I had been, still trying to delude myself that I was controlling the story. I wasn't, not any more. And it was all my own fault. I had given him the plot, and here I was, trapped in it. There was only one speech left for me to make.

"You are right," I said with a sigh, "that in one respect I cannot hope to compete with Jean. But I wish her no ill. Can't I convince you of that? And if I did, I wouldn't use

such a crude way of trying to get rid of her. It's my books
I'm worried about at the moment. Truly it is.''

I stopped. This was the moment for an appealing gesture,
a touch on his arm, a fervent gaze into his eyes. The mere
thought of it revolted me. I continued to grip the back of the
settee; he continued to lean forward in his armchair. We
stared at each other.

"I just wondered," I said feebly, "whether Jean might
perhaps have an idea who else could have taken the typescripts. I don't mean that she isn't extremely careful and conscientious, but one can never be sure—there are always
people—gasmen, for instance, someone coming to read the
meter—''

I broke off: I had been about to add "A policeman calling
over a supposed parking offence," but decided it would be
safer at this point not to mention the law.

Brent sauntered confidently down the trail that he had
forced me to open up for him.

"You've got to be very careful nowadays," he agreed,
"about whom you let into your house. Yes, certainly, I'll
have a word with Jean. She might remember if there was
anything in the least suspicious. And you're not forgetting, I
hope, that Mrs. Simmonds was still around for a day or two
after we went away? Not to mention that nosy neighbour of
ours. He's been poking around here a lot, apparently. Jean
didn't like it at all. Not at all.''

He played with his glass before taking another drink; the
picture of a law-abiding citizen shaking his head over the
wickedness of the world.

"You'll ask her, then?" I said. "I think it will come better
from you. She seems to be rather shy with me.''

He laughed again. "Jealousy, the green-eyed monster.
You're not the only one suffering from it.''

I could not answer this; I was feeling very sick again and
it was a relief when he put down his glass for the last time
and said: "Oughtn't we to be working? What are your next
instructions, ma'am?''

It was a measure of the hatefulness of my present situation
that I regarded it as a great blessing that I was able to avoid
any further physical contact with him for the moment. But
this was the only reason I had to be thankful. They presented

an impregnable front, the two of them, Jean and her silence and Brent now skilfully turning against me all the weapons I had given him. Direct attack was no use; if I was to make any headway it would have to be by some more subtle means.

"Fortunately," I said to Brent later that day after he had informed me that Jean knew nothing whatever about the missing manuscripts, "fortunately I still have the original handwritten draft of one of the novels. Miss Gray and I came across it when we were searching. Of course I altered it a lot later, but it should still be possible to write up a fair approximation to the missing script."

I watched him as I spoke—he was as usual helping himself to sherry—and I felt sure that these remarks had given him a jolt. He could hardly ask which book, because he was not supposed to know anything of the contents of either of them, and even if he suspected that I was bluffing and that there was no such handwritten draft, still he could not be sure. If he really was plotting to make use of my books, then he would need to get hold of the draft and of anything I might write up from it, and in this way I ought to be able to tempt him out into the open.

When Marian came to hear the outcome of my talk with Brent I made a great deal of this idea of mine and played down the humiliation I had suffered earlier on.

"But have you really got an early draft?" she asked.

"No. I threw them all away."

"Then how long will it take you to produce something that looks authentic enough for him?"

"About a week, at least," I replied, and at the thought of the labour involved, my enthusiasm for the scheme began to wane. If I put my mind to it I could remember quite a lot of the content of the two missing novels, but I had not the least desire to re-write either of them. I wanted to write again, but not in that style. Was it worth it? After all, it was primarily the diaries, and not the novels, that I was so desperately anxious to retrieve. But I could not tell Marian that.

"Shall you let him see you writing?" she asked. "Or do you intend to wait until you have a few chapters ready and put them in a prominent place before leaving him alone in the room?"

"The latter," I said lamely, "was rather what I had in mind."

"But he'd never be fool enough to take them. And even if you *did* surprise him reading them—well, he'd have plenty of foolproof excuses ready, wouldn't he?"

"I suppose so. Oh, let's forget it, Marian. It won't work. It's a feeble sort of scheme."

But she wouldn't leave it alone and I was obliged to listen for what seemed hours to her various ideas for trapping Brent, some of them quite reasonable, others ludicrous. She was genuinely anxious to help and she was sorry for me in a somewhat contemptuous way, but she was also thoroughly enjoying herself.

"The trouble is, Nell," she said, "that he'll never feel really safe—safe to produce your books as if they were his own. Not while you're alive, at any rate."

"Well that's all that interests me. He can do what he likes after I'm dead, which won't be just yet, I hope. Philip and Dora will lose the proceeds of two of my books, but I can't say that worries me greatly. Now what's the matter, Marian? Why are you looking at me like that? What have I said?"

She was indeed staring at me with a most extraordinary expression on her face.

"After you're dead," she said. "Good God, let's hope it doesn't come to that!"

Marian was a sober person, not given to hysterics and to false alarms. The thought was all the more chilling, stated in her matter-of-fact voice.

"I wish you hadn't told him you were going to re-write one of the books," she said. "It might give him ideas."

"Well, I can't unsay it now. Oh do shut up, Marian. He's not going to murder me."

"I don't want to be alarmist, but I must point out that people have been killed for far less money than will accrue from even one of your books. Not to mention the fame, which you say he craves for."

"But how?" I expostulated. "It's hard enough getting rid of people in books, let alone in real life."

"Nevertheless it is happening every day."

"Oh yes—muggings and family brawls. Not cases where it's essential not to be detected."

"I don't like you being here alone with them," said Marian, getting up. "I think I had better move in for a while."

"As food-taster?" I mocked. "In case Jean sends me up a cup of poisoned coffee?"

"It could happen," said Marian stolidly.

13

For the next couple of weeks I was very glad of Marian's company. Whether or not she was saving me from being murdered, at least she protected me from Brent, and the fact that he was clearly frustrated and annoyed showed that he had not anticipated this counter move. As soon as he came upstairs for the morning's instructions Marian would retire to the kitchen, leaving the communicating door with the big drawing-room slightly ajar, and every now and then announcing her continued presence by means of a little rattle of cutlery or the click of a cupboard door.

"For Christ's sake," said Brent to me on the third morning, under cover of the noise of the washing machine, "is she cooking a banquet or something?"

He leaned forward: "Helen—am I never going to get you to myself?"

I shrugged my shoulders and made a grimace indicating hopeless resignation.

"I can't stop her," I said. "She's determined to act chaperone."

At the next opportunity he said: "If you want help with the housework, you know, Jean would be only too pleased to do it in her free time. And she'd do it well too. I wish you'd let her. We feel we owe you so much—both of us—that we'd like to take this chance of repaying you."

The hypocrisy of this revolted me and his ingratiating smile looked to me more like a sinister leer. Had it not been for

Marian plodding about next door, I should have felt quite frightened. Frightened enough to do what he asked and let Jean have the full run of my home again. As it was, I was able to say quite calmly that I would be glad to take up the offer eventually but that for the moment I had better not offend Marian. However, I could not expect her to act as watchdog for ever and I was beginning to consider other long-term possibilities when something happened that drastically changed the whole situation.

Marian had been persuaded to go out for the evening, and would not be back until very late. It was the annual dinner of her photographic club, to which she looked forward all the year and which she had heroically offered to miss, but I promised her that the moment she had gone I would bolt the front door and not open it to Brent or to anyone else but herself.

"But what are you going to do," she wanted to know, "if he calls up on the phone and says he's simply got to see you? You're going to weaken, Nell, and let him in."

"No, I'm not," I retorted. "I'm much too scared of him now. *You*'ve seen to that."

It comforted me a little to pretend that Marian was being alarmist in attributing evil intentions to Brent, but in truth I greatly disliked the thought of being alone in the house with him and as soon as she had gone I did exactly as I said I would. When I got upstairs again the phone was ringing. It could well have been from the basement flat and I lifted the receiver, assembling all my strength, and telling myself that it did not matter what foolish excuse I gave so long as I did not let him in.

But it was a woman's voice on the line. Not Jean's; a much louder, more confident voice, familiar to me but for the moment I could not place it.

"Mrs. Simmonds!" I cried at last. "How lovely to hear from you! How are you getting on? Where are you? Can you talk?"

Yes, she could talk; she was at her daughter's, and we began to chat away like long lost sisters.

"Now that's enough about me," I said after giving her a cheerful account of the public side of my recent tour. "What about you? Do you like the job?"

Oh yes, it was very interesting; you really felt as if you

were at the centre of things. She was kept terribly busy; she
would have phoned before but she hardly had a moment to
call her own and had to cancel her last day off because of
unexpected overseas visitors.

Lady Walters? Oh yes, she was all right so long as you
gave her no excuse for complaining. And Lord Walters? Oh,
he was delightful. Most charming and friendly. It was impossible not to like him. Hadn't I found him a very delightful
person?

Cautiously I replied that I had always got on with him very
well and then, as Mrs. Simmonds obviously expected a fuller
comment, I added that he had been an interesting and stim-
ulating person to work with because he was so full of vitality
and new ideas. This reply was more to her liking and she
launched forth into a eulogy of Barry to which I listened with
mixed feelings. From what she said and from my recollections of him it seemed as if he had been going out of his way
to make a good impression on her and I wondered about his
motive. It might simply be that as he grew older he grew
more dependent on women's admiration. Or it might be due
to Mrs. Simmonds's connection with myself; in some curious
way he might feel that by charming Mrs. Simmonds he was
getting at me, showing me that other people valued him even
if I didn't.

The thought was gratifying but also disturbing; the temptation to pump Mrs. Simmonds was irresistible.

"I hope you'll give me a rave reference if he ever asks
about me," I said laughingly.

She replied in all earnestness: "He thinks the world of
you. There's a shelf of your books in the library and I've
heard him recommending them to guests. And he's asked
about you—do you travel much, do you entertain much—that
sort of thing."

"Really? What did you reply?"

I tried to speak as lightly as before but it wasn't easy.

"I told him how much I admired you and had enjoyed
working for you," said Mrs. Simmonds in her most down-
right way. "But I'm ever so glad to hear you are well, Miss
Mitchell, because several times during the last day or two
Lord Walters has mentioned your health and asked me
whether you were subject to nervous troubles of any kind and

I was so worried because I thought perhaps he might have some information that I didn't. Of course I told him you were perfectly all right, but I was worried all the same, because I knew how tired you were before you went away.''

''I was indeed, and I'm afraid I was very tiresome and obstinate, as over-tired people are apt to be. But I am perfectly well now, Mrs. Simmonds. Honestly I am.''

''I believe you,'' she said. ''I can tell you are. I can hear it in your voice.''

It was nice to have such warm confirmation of my return to sanity, but apart from that Mr. Simmonds's last statements had made me uneasy and I was even more troubled when she said: ''Mind you, he's not been himself at all these last few days. Lady Walters says she has never seen him so depressed and she can't understand why, because everything is going very well at the moment and there's no particular cause for concern so far as she knows.''

''Perhaps he isn't well,'' I suggested.

''That's what I said,'' returned Mrs. Simmonds, ''but apparently he gets very impatient if anyone suggests he is doing too much.''

We talked a little longer and arranged to meet for lunch one day.

My fingers were just about to let go of the receiver when I remembered my present predicament, which the conversation with Mrs. Simmonds had temporarily driven from my mind. Brent might well have been trying to get through while we were talking; let him go on thinking that the number was engaged. I laid the receiver on the low table and moved to my desk and sat down in the swivel chair. There was a pen and scrap paper lying on the blotter and my hands reached towards them as if drawn by a magnet. I was conscious of nothing but the great anxiety and unease which the warmth of Mrs. Simmonds's voice had momentarily dispelled, but some power outside myself seemed to have taken over my mind and hand and I was helpless to resist. I didn't even know what the next sentence was going to be until I saw it forming.

After a while it came to an end, not abruptly, but kindly and gently, as if to say: now that's enough for this time. I had covered several sheets of foolscap and with great trepidation I began to read. Probably it would be nonsense, like examination papers written under the influence of pep drugs, or like those solutions to the mystery of the universe that come with startling clarity in dreams, only to dissolve into meaningless syllables at the moment of waking.

It was not exactly nonsense but it was very odd: intense, rambling, apocalyptic stuff about forgiveness and redemption; about its being hate and not love that makes the world go round—hate, the great driving force which spares no human creature, for every man, however self-sufficient, must have an enemy, someone to blame for the trials of his life and the ills of the world. But most of all we hate ourselves, and the Christian command to "love your enemies" was a command to make friends with ourselves.

That part of the manuscript was a straightforward statement of belief, but elsewhere there were characters and dialogue. The characters had names like "The Friend," "The Foe," and "The Forgiver." What a lot of effs, as Brent would say.

I read it through again and this time it seemed like a not very efficient lesson in a religious instruction series. If this was new model Helen Mitchell then she was going to be lucky to find a publisher, let alone a wide readership. It might, however, provide the theme for a novel.

I sat thinking how this might be done and for the first time since my return from Germany I found myself becoming so deeply absorbed that all anxiety and fear faded completely away and the sense of the book to be written took over the whole of my being. Hatred and resentment, forgiveness and acceptance—these were the key concepts, and the people who were to exemplify them gradually began to emerge from the primal mist.

With shattering, agonizing irrelevance the sound of the front door bell broke into my thoughts and for a few moments I sat bewildered, unable to comprehend the noise. The bell rang again. I stretched out a hand and drew aside the curtain a little. The glimpse of the brightly lit promenade restored me to time and circumstance. It was ten minutes past ten. I switched on the centre light and the room instantly became a public place. Then I lifted the speaker of the intercom.

"Who is that, please?"

The reply was inaudible, which was reassuring, since had it been Brent he would instantly have made himself clear.

"Would you please talk directly into the small grating alongside the bell," I said. "I can't hear you otherwise."

This time the reply was audible, but very low:

"The name is Walters."

"I'll be right down," I said. "It's no use pushing the knob because I have to unbolt the door."

I was absolutely calm, frozen calm, and as I came downstairs I focused my thoughts on the manner of his arrival. Had he left the car a little distance away and walked the last few yards? Was he alone? Was his detective lurking behind the bushes in the little garden? Had he been seen—either by Brent or by anybody else?

The bolts were heavy and stiff and difficult to shift.

"I'm sorry to be such an age," were my first words when at last I had succeeded in opening the door. "I've only recently begun to use these bolts."

"They need oiling," he said as he stepped across the threshold.

"I know they do," I said irritably.

Fifteen years!—and yet in the very first second of our reunion I was apologizing where I might well have expected an apology, and he was walking through the hall as if the house belonged to him.

"Upstairs?" he asked, glancing back at me over his shoulder.

"Yes."

He put a foot on the bottom stair and then remembered to draw back and let me lead the way. He panted a little at the end of the first flight and I paused on the half-landing to let him recover.

"Nice house," he said in a condescending manner. "How much did you give for it?"

I told him the figure.

"You'd get four times that now. More still if sold in separate units."

I moved on again without replying. Shock, nostalgia, apprehension—all the appropriate reactions were swallowed up in petty annoyance: why did he keep telling me what I knew perfectly well already? As if I couldn't follow trends in the real estate market as well as he. He was heavy and short of breath and I was lined and greying, but it was the same between us as it had always been. The years had altered nothing. If I had been Prime Minister and he the dustman it would have been just the same. We irritated each other; we knew each other through and through and yet we could never truly meet.

When we reached the drawing-room I poured him whisky without asking if he wanted it.

"I oughtn't to have this," he said.

"Oh?" This was new. "Medical advice? Or public relations? I hadn't noticed you were projecting a teetotal image."

"I've got angina," he said in a dejected way. "It's quite serious."

Instantly I was overcome with remorse.

"I'm terribly sorry, Barry."

"The best policy is not to take too much notice of it," he replied, side-stepping so that my sympathy overshot its mark. "One has to learn to live with it. It's an attitude of mind."

He drained his glass and looked at me. There was a pasty and unhealthy tinge in his skin but the blue-grey eyes were as alert as ever.

"Do you keep well, Helen? You certainly look very well. Middle-aged poise suits you."

Typical Barry again. A carefully measured ration of concern for the other person, just enough to show them that he was not entirely self-centred, but woe to anybody who took it as an invitation to expand upon their own affairs. Down would come the guillotine—politely and ruthlessly.

"I'm very well, thank you," I said. "Just returned from a very pleasant working holiday."

"Good, good."

That was enough of that. I waited.

"Very efficient woman, Mrs. Simmonds," was his next remark.

I agreed wholeheartedly. "She was wasting her talents, just looking after me."

This was the sort of remark that he never bothered to hear.

"Her references," he went on, "when she first came to you. Were they all right? Nothing at all suspicious?"

"Good heavens, no!" I exclaimed. "She'd worked mainly

in colleges and similar places. Didn't you write to her previous employers?''

"Of course. She was once in charge of a directors' diningroom in the City, wasn't she?''

"I believe so. She didn't like it much. Too hierarchical. A good salary, but no one ever spoke to her as if she were a human being. What is the matter, Barry? Is Mrs. Simmonds in some sort of trouble?''

I nearly mentioned that I had just been speaking to her but decided against it until I knew the real reason for Barry's visit.

"I don't suppose for a moment that it has anything to do with her,'' he was saying, "but all the same it is odd that it has only cropped up since she came.''

"What has, Barry?''

I took a sip of brandy to try to steady my nerves, to check the chill trembling of apprehension. For I knew now, as surely as one knows when somebody says "I'm afraid I have bad news,'' that something horrible and inescapable was about to come.

He took an envelope out of a wallet and handed it to me.

"You're the mystery-monger, Helen. What do you make of this?''

It was a small manilla envelope with the address typed in double-spacing too near the bottom—a minor error of judgment to which I myself was very prone. In the top left-hand corner was typed "Personal and Strictly Private'', twice underlined, and the stamp had been crookedly affixed, with one corner peeling off where the gum had been insufficiently moistened. Another tendency of mine. The postmark was Brighton, the date too blurred to decipher.

I opened the envelope and drew out a single quarto sheet of thin typing paper—the sort I myself use for carbons. The message was in double-spacing, adequately but not faultlessly typed in the small, well-spaced lettering of a Speedway portable—the same model as my own. The letter "a" was slightly out of alignment and often had a faint ghost of itself a fraction to the right, as if the key was apt to stick and hover over the paper instead of hitting it sharply. This fault was a common one on Speedway portables; my own machine was no exception.

My eye and mind dwelt on these details, studying the message as if it were in a foreign language, deliberately refusing to understand its meaning as I sometimes did when a bad review caused me pain.

"I get a lot of anonymous letters," said Barry. "Always abusive and sometimes obscene. Usually one of my secretaries disposes of them. This one I happened to open myself. It came to my private address two days ago. It seems to be in a different category from the usual stuff. Rather more disturbing for that very reason."

"Yes indeed," I said vaguely, scarcely hearing him, but conscious that I could no longer avoid taking in the sense of the words.

"You hypocrite," it ran, "have you no sense of shame?

"Cushioned in luxury, wallowing in self-righteousness— do you ever remember who it was who put you there? Do you ever recall other people's lives, stunted and sterile, sacrificed on the altar of your success? Why should they keep silent any longer, those whose lives you have swallowed up and then cast off when they could be exploited no more? Why shouldn't they prick the bubble—let the world know the source of your ill-gotten gains? A word to the editor of *Zoom-Lens* would see it published in an early issue. They aren't afraid of libel; they have cut other inflated reputations down to size. Don't you think you deserve it?"

I let the paper fall on my lap and reached out again for the brandy glass.

"You see what I mean," said Barry. "No crudities, no spelling mistakes, and some pretensions to a literary style. Yet no demand for cash. Presumably that will come later. Well? What do you make of it?"

I couldn't look at him and I couldn't speak. I replaced my glass on the table and read the message again.

". . . stunted and sterile . . . sacrificed on the altar . . . ill-gotten gains . . ."

No, I would never have written such stuff, not even in that state of mental confusion in which I believed myself to have posted a parcel which in fact I never sent. Besides, that incident had taken place weeks ago, whereas the anonymous letter had been posted very recently. Before I went away I might just conceivably have written it, but not after my return. At no point since the moment when I entered my drawing-room with Brent and Jean following close behind me had I been overcome by the sort of bitterness and despair that alone could lead to threatening a man's whole future. I had been excessively worried about the missing papers but I had been thoroughly alive to what was going on around me, and on the one occasion when I had allowed my subconscious mind to guide my pen the result had been the extraordinary rigmarole about redemption and forgiveness—a far cry from vindictive anonymous letters.

I had not written this letter to Barry; I was absolutely sure of that.

But Barry evidently suspected that I had and this suspicion had driven him to arrive on my doorstep, unannounced, after our long separation. I played for time.

"It looks like my typewriter, but there are many similar, and I can hardly believe that Mrs. Simmonds—" I paused for a moment before asking: "What makes you think she might be involved?"

"Opportunity mostly. She'd been close to you for some time. I thought it just possible that she might somehow have come to learn—"

He left the sentence unfinished. He was looking away from me, evidently reluctant to make a direct accusation, but whether for my sake or for his own I could not tell.

"Of course it is just possible that she might have picked up something when she worked in the City and put two and two together," he said.

"I'm sure you can rule out Mrs. Simmonds," I said as firmly as I could. "Isn't there anyone else who might be responsible? Someone working with you at the time?"

"They're all dead," he said. "The few who could possibly know. Except perhaps that woman who was working for Cooper—the whole enterprise was his brainchild, you remember—pity he never lived to enjoy the best of it. I don't think he told her very much, though. She didn't stay with him very long. She married a chartered accountant a good many years older than herself."

My heart gave a little leap. Could there possibly be a link with Mr. Thorburn?

"Emigrated to Australia," Barry was saying. "Name of Sanderson."

No, of course there was no tie-up with my elderly neighbour who had had access to my house. This was the sort of red herring that I might use myself to spin out the story a little longer. But it was no longer my story; another mind had taken over the plot.

"Barry," I said suddenly, interrupting him, "how serious could this be? I mean, could anything really be proved against you now, even if *Zoom-Lens* did get hold of it?"

"It couldn't be worse," he replied. "If *Zoom-Lens* gets even a sniff of it I'm done for."

And he proceeded to give particulars of eminent persons whose past indiscretions had been investigated by that indefatigable journal and whose careers had never recovered from it.

"But Barry," I said very tentatively, "does it really matter so very much to you now? I mean, you wanted to get to the top and you've done it. I assume you didn't want to be PM or you wouldn't have taken a peerage. So what else do you want? Surely you have enough money to live in luxury for the rest of your days, and as for the adulation, does it still mean so very much to you? If your heart's in a bad way wouldn't it be a good idea to retire?"

"I can't retire," he said impatiently. "I've got too many irons in the fire. And it gets a grip on you. Once you get on the treadmill you can't get off it."

The treadmill! I had been on one too, and I had escaped it. But at a very great cost.

"Besides," he added, "it's not just a question of resigning my office or even of social ostracism. This is Criminal Court stuff, Helen. You don't know the half of it."

"You could be prosecuted?" I asked slowly. "You could actually end up in prison?"

"Yes," he replied simply. "I wouldn't be the first. That shakes you, doesn't it, Helen?"

I covered my face with my hands. "Your wife," I muttered through my fingers. "Does she know?"

"Rita would hate it if I retired," he said. "She hasn't seen this letter. And she doesn't know anything. I have always made sure of that. If she knows nothing she can give nothing away. I confide in no woman. I never have confided in any woman but you."

He was dropping broader and broader hints about his suspicion of me. Soon it would be out in the open and I still did not know how I was going to respond. I was too agitated to sit still any longer and I got up from my chair, pushing it back as I did so. The movement must have exposed the low table with the telephone on it to Barry's gaze, because he said: "Did you know your receiver was off? No wonder I couldn't get through when I phoned."

I exclaimed in surprise and then began to apologize.

"It's very wrong of me," I said, "but I was writing and didn't want to be interrupted."

There seemed nothing for it but to replace the receiver. Surely Brent would not ring now. I leaned over the telephone, with my back to Barry. Should I try to prop it up somehow so that he would not notice the receiver was not firmly replaced? Or make some excuse to run upstairs so that I could cut off the outside line on the extension in my bedroom?

I heard movement behind me and I lifted the phone and made a great show of disentangling the knots in the wire. But Barry had gone to my desk and was turning over the handwritten pages that lay on the blotter.

"I'm sorry I interrupted you," he muttered, not looking at me. "I know how annoying it is when one is concentrating on a job."

I stared at him, unable to speak, and for the first time since he had come into the house I really saw him. Tall and upright as ever, carrying too much weight but still not quite offensively obese. Hair greying, thinning a little on the forehead; hands very well cared for. Conventionally and expensively dressed—no attempt to be trendy. A prosperous citizen, worthy but dull. What had become of all the life and the fire? He was nervous in my presence. In spite of all my agitation I had somehow succeeded in subduing him with the Helen Mitchell persona. He had actually apologized—an unheard of thing in our previous relationship.

"You write in longhand, do you?" he went on, still avoiding my eye. "You find that more satisfactory?"

"Yes," I replied.

"But surely you get someone to type the final copy?"

"Yes. I have a secretary."

I dared not say more. Did he know about Brent? What had
Mrs. Simmonds told him?

"You really need someone living in," he said, "to protect
you from phone calls and suchlike."

"Marian Gray—you may remember her?—is staying with
me, but she is out tonight. And I am going abroad again
soon, and on my return shall move into a smaller house. Mrs.
Simmonds may have mentioned this to you."

He turned over the papers again and said in a voice so low
that I could only just catch the words: "So you never married."

I could not reply.

Suddenly he raised his head and looked straight at me, the
eyes very wide open, very hopeless, very appealing.

"Help me, Helen. I beg you. For old time's sake."

"I—I—" I swallowed and tried again. "This prosecution
risk, would that be over the People's Park deal? Or something
else?"

"Oh, for Christ's sake! I wish I hadn't told you. Now you're
going to nag. You always did nag me, Helen."

He flung down my manuscript and returned to his place
on the settee.

"Nag you?" I echoed. "I'm sure I never nagged."

"Not in words maybe. But you looked it all the time. Silently criticizing. Used to get on my nerves sometimes."

"But why didn't you tell me so, Barry? I never knew, I
never realized."

"Oh well." He shrugged. "Didn't want to upset you."

I sat down, trying to take this in.

"And Rita," I said when I could command my voice.
"Rita doesn't nag—doesn't get upset?"

"Oh lord yes. She nags. But in a different way. She wants
a new car, she thinks I ought to diet—that sort of thing. She's
a greedy bitch. But she doesn't get upset. And I don't have
to live up to her."

"I see," I said quietly.

So it was as simple as that. All he had wanted was a woman
he could have rows with—a stupid, demanding woman who
would behave as a traditional nagging wife. He didn't want
an equal partner; he wanted someone at whom he could throw

all his frustrations, someone to complain about, someone to blame. Just like Brent. "The old woman won't let me." "I'll have to ask the missus." Those would be the sort of phrases he would have uttered had he remained in the society into which he and Brent had been born. My wonderful, big-thinking superman—nothing but a would-be henpecked husband. Had I been creating fiction even before I began to write it? My irresistible Barry—was he my own invention? And had I carried over my illusions on to the other, on to Brent?

"Poor Barry," I said, half-laughing, "were you really so much in awe of me? It's hard to believe."

"And I find it hard to believe that you—"

He broke off and again called up the desperate look into his eyes.

"Sitting there so cool and collected," he went on, "not giving a damn for anybody. It's incredible that you could ever feel strongly enough to do such a thing and yet if it wasn't you—"

"To do what thing, Barry?" I asked steadily, and while I waited for him to reply I was thinking: they all say I am unfeeling; could they be right and I myself wrong? Is this tumult within myself ever concerned with other people, or is it an internal drama, the power-house of my writing? Do I indeed care for nobody?

"This damned letter." Barry looked at me appealingly. "Did you write it?"

I thought very hard before replying.

"Will it make you feel better if I say I did?"

He made an impatient noise. "The point is—did you or didn't you?"

I turned my head aside, hoping he would take the gesture for a silent confession.

"I quite understand," he said heavily, "that you might feel you were hardly done by by me. We should never have made a go of it together, but that's not the point. The point is that you don't really want to muck up my whole career, do you, Helen? What is there in it for you? You don't need money and you above all people would get no kick out of revenge."

"I'm not in a position to endanger your career," I said. "I don't possess any information that could be damaging to you."

He snatched at this eagerly; it was pathetic to watch.

"Don't you? Are you sure? I didn't think you could, but there was an outside chance. Then you just wanted to give me a fright? Well you've done that all right." He laughed, but it rang very false. "Don't do it again; there's a good girl. Please promise me, Helen."

I said nothing.

"You did write it, didn't you?" There was sharp anxiety in his voice. "Please answer me. I know you won't tell me a lie."

I replied at last, picking my words with very great care:

"I can truthfully say, Barry, that I am responsible for the writing of that letter."

He let out breath noisily.

"That's a relief. And you won't send any more?"

"I will do my very best to see that you get no more."

"Do your best!" he cried. "D'you mean to say you can't stop yourself? Or don't know you're doing it? Have you gone mad or something?"

"Sometimes I think I have."

"Then you'd better take yourself off to a psychiatrist and get him to stop you writing anonymous letters. But don't tell him who they are to or what they're about."

He was very jittery now, more so than he had been since his arrival, and he was making no secret of his feeling of antagonism towards me. But then he thought me guilty of a vicious and despicable act, in which case I could hardly deserve kindness. I was glad he believed me; it had been my intention to set his mind at rest by convincing him that I alone, and no other, was responsible for the threat. Nevertheless it was painful to be treated in this way. Suddenly I thought of those tragic heroines, such as Camille, who sacrificed everything, including even their lovers' good opinion of them, in order to save their lovers from some danger.

I tried to laugh the notion away, reminding myself that I was not an injured innocent but that my own carelessness had enabled somebody else to threaten Barry. It was no use. The comparison would persist, and then illumination struck me as we stood in the front hall, awkwardly bidding each other goodnight. I had every right to be compared with such a heroine because I too was going to sacrifice myself. I was

going to make sure that Barry would be troubled no further;
I was going to silence the person or persons who were threatening him and I was going to stick at nothing to achieve this
end.

My hand was on the door-knob.

"Where is your car?" I asked.

"Cruising round the block. They'll pick me up round the
corner."

He was breathing unevenly again; even walking downstairs
had tired him and his face looked paler than ever. The visit
had been a great strain for him. Or perhaps he was a lot more
ill than he had admitted. My heart contracted with tenderness
and I longed to make some sign of it. But affectionate cos-
seting was not my role; I had bigger things to do. And in any
case he would not tolerate it from me. He thought I was out
of my mind, and the fact that this distressed him showed that
he must retain some feeling for me. But he was also very
puzzled because my behaviour was not that of an unbalanced
person.

"Goodbye then," I said, seeking to get rid of him before
he began to suspect that my "confession" was a lie. "I hope
you won't be troubled by any more letters but it's just possible
that there is another on the way. If so, just ring me up and
let me know what it says. There's no need to worry. That
will be the end of it."

"I should hope so indeed. Extraordinary business."

I opened the door and he walked through without saying
goodbye. Then he turned round, stepped back into the hall
and caught my arm:

"Helen," he said in an exasperated tone, "do go to that
doctor. You're obviously not yourself. It's quite unlike you to
let your feelings get the better of you—particularly such stupid and unproductive feelings. You've probably been overworking. Or it might be your age—change of life—that sort
of thing."

His voice softened and he looked at me appealingly:

"It must be that, mustn't it? You don't really wish me any
harm?"

"No, no!" I cried, twisting my hands together and shaking
my head. "I don't wish you any harm. I couldn't bear anything to happen to you. You *must* believe me—you *must*!"

"Yes, yes. Now don't get upset." He patted my shoulder.
"Yes, yes, Helen. Of course I believe you. I must go now.
Good night."

This time he did not turn back and I stood in the doorway
watching him walk slowly down the shallow steps, moving
his head from side to side as a gesture of his continued puzzlement. He turned into the side road at the end of the terrace
and I waited a few minutes in case the big dark car emerged
on to the promenade. But it must have gone the other way.
All that happened was a movement in the area below—the
door of the basement flat was opening. Hastily I shut my own
front door, shot the bolts, switched off the hall light and crept
upstairs in the half-darkness. When I came to the drawing-
room I turned off the lights, felt my way to the settee and
sank down at the corner where Barry had been sitting.

And that was all I could manage. I leaned back against the
cushions and the tears came like spring rain—fifteen seasons
of them—never stopping, never increasing, just falling steadily on and on. It was all so utterly simple and yet I had never
understood it before. I loved Barry, whatever he was, who-
ever he was, and whatever he thought of me.

I had been madly possessive about him during all that time
when I had believed myself to be devoting my whole life to
his advancement and I had thought it was love. But it wasn't.
It was nothing to what I felt now. For I had no bitterness
now, no jealousy, no need even to be loved and appreciated
in return. It didn't matter that he thought me mad, that I
might never hear another kind word from him, never see him
again. All that mattered was to silence his attacker. It would
require every bit of my skill and ingenuity but I would ac-
complish it somehow. It seemed as if all my imaginative gifts
and my long experience in story-telling, my capacity for spinning a plot and my ability to devise methods of killing, were
but a prelude, a trial run for the carrying out of this one object;
as if my whole life had been leading up to this one moment,
that alone gave meaning and purpose to all that had gone before.

14

Poor Marian had to ring the bell again and again before it penetrated my consciousness. And then I staggered drunkenly to the intercom and said: "Who's that?"

My voice came out in a harsh croak.

"Nell! Is that you? What on earth's the matter?" cried Marian.

"I'm all right." It was a bit clearer this time. "Got a frightful cold coming on. I'll be down in a moment."

But I went first into the kitchen and splashed water over my face. Then I found a handkerchief and practised sneezing. It sounded quite convincing, and I managed several loud ones immediately after opening the door to Marian.

"Shut it quick," I gasped, wiping my eyes with the handkerchief. "The cold air starts me off again."

Ten minutes later she was dosing me with her favourite cold remedies and we were exclaiming over its sudden onset and the virulence of its symptoms.

"You did give me a fright," she said. "You sounded awful. I thought for a moment I was going to find you half-strangled."

"Oh no," I replied. "No drama at all this evening. Not a sign of Brent. I've been writing a bit. How did the dinner go?"

I pressed her to tell me about her evening in order to avoid further questioning. But I need not have worried. Marian was somewhat tiddly and very full of the occasion. Somebody had been admiring one of her recent photographs and she had promised to let him have some spare copies as soon as she had time, but she had explained that she was rather tied up at the moment.

"That settles it," I cried. "You're going home tomorrow to get on with your own affairs. I've taken quite enough of your time. I shall go up to Phil's for a few days. Actually I've thought of a solution to my problem but I won't explain to-night because we're both of us nearly asleep."

I did not sleep, however, but lay much of the night propped up against the pillows, with the bedside lamp on and a pencil and pad lying near to hand. My mind was very active and every now and then I would jot down a few notes.

In the morning I told Marian that my cold was much better and that I was going to carry out the first part of my scheme. But I wanted her out of the way when Brent came up for the morning's work.

"I shall stay upstairs," she said. "He need not know I'm here."

At half past nine Brent knocked on the drawing-room door.

"She's gone? Thank God," he said, miming exaggerated relief when he saw that I was alone. "She scares me, your girl-friend."

He leaned over the back of my chair—I was seated at the desk—and his lips touched my hair. I said nothing.

"All ready for work, are we? No dalliance this morning either?"

He was very nervous. This was a good sign. I made a motion for him to sit down and prepare to receive instructions, hoping that this very cool reception would drive him to burst out with something of his own accord.

I had not judged wrong.

"Lot of telephoning going on last night, wasn't there?" he said. "I tried nonstop for an hour to get you—just to see if you were all right without your chaperone. We were quite worried when we found the line always engaged—and that you had barricaded yourself in too."

He broke off and looked at me, all features working. I simply raised my eyebrows.

"Thought you might have felt life wasn't worth living after

losing your brain-child," he went on. "I half expected to be rousing the suicide rescue squad this morning."

"Are you ready for dictation?" I asked.

I was not conscious of looking and sounding supremely contemptuous but I must have done so because he went very red, as he had often done in the early days of our close acquaintanceship.

"Oh, it's like that, is it? We're a great lady this morning. All right. You're the boss. Go ahead."

He picked up a notebook and pen. He had a smattering of shorthand from his few months as a reporter—not very speedy but it had proved adequate for our purposes.

"This will be the notes for my next novel," I said. "Mrs. Fairbrother used to type out three copies—one for my publisher, one for my agent, and the third for my guidance while working on the first draft of the book. They should be double-spaced, with wide margins and an inch between each paragraph. Are you ready? Provisional title—'Plot Counter-plot; Characters'—list these downwards, please, as in a theatre programme—'in order of appearance: Louise, a novelist; Mrs. Prettyman, her housekeeper-oblique-confidante; Stephen, another novelist'."

At this point I thought I heard him give an involuntary exclamation but I ignored it and continued, glancing at the handwritten notes that I had made during the night:

" 'Bertha, Louise's friend; Mr. Dooley, her neighbour; Thomas, her brother; Sonia, Stephen's mistress; Sir Graham Reeves, a public figure; and various minor characters'—type that on a separate line at the bottom. 'The scene is an elegant town house in a fashionable resort on the South Coast of England. Time—the present.' I'm sorry, am I going too fast?"

He had exclaimed again; he was reacting even sooner than I had hoped. I studied my notes, pretending that I was waiting for him to catch up with his shorthand writing. As on a former occasion, I was intensely conscious of every movement he made, every breath he drew.

"Shall I go on?" I said, when it looked as if his breakdown was not going to come quite yet.

He muttered something inaudibly.

" 'The story opens with Louise re-reading her old diaries, written during the heyday of her love affair with Sir Graham, and comparing those days with the dreariness of her present life. Mrs. Prettyman serves to set the scene and establish Louise's status. Enter Stephen, seeking help for his own lack of inspiration and exercising all his charm. Louise falls for him.' I beg your pardon, did you speak, Brent?''

He had thrown his pen on the floor; he banged with the flat of his hand on the table at which he was sitting.

"Look here, Helen," he exclaimed. "If this is meant to be a joke then I don't think it's very funny, and if you are trying to tell me something then wouldn't it be quicker to do it straight out instead of in this roundabout way?"

"This is no joke," I said. "I am planning a novel. This is the way I usually set about it."

"But the characters—the whole set-up. Good God, d'you mean to say you really *were* planning to use that starting-off point—you and me—our first meeting—that you suggested *I* should base my next book on?"

"Of course. I have been thinking out how a story might develop from that given situation. Haven't you? I thought you were well on with yours, although you didn't want me to see any of it beyond the first chapter or two. You did go on writing, didn't you? Or have you only been pretending to me that you did?"

"Yes, I did go on writing," he said angrily.

"And so did I. Or rather, I didn't actually write, but I thought about it, and now it has reached the point of letting my agent and publisher see a summary so that they know what to expect. This is my normal procedure."

It wasn't, of course. I never told anybody what the next book was to be about. The first person to know anything had been Mrs. Fairbrother when she typed the final draft, and in the case of the missing novels I had typed that myself.

But Brent believed me and he was very rattled.

"Had they been sent summaries of the typescripts that you have lost?" he asked.

"As far as I can remember, yes, they had, although I cannot put my hand on the carbon copies at the moment. Anyway, I can soon write up a summary from my early draft, but I don't want to be bothered with those books at the moment. I would prefer to make a start on this new novel. Shall we go on?"

"All right."

He found another pen and poised himself to write, but I didn't expect to get very far before there came another outburst.

" 'Louise, in her passion for Stephen, loses her head completely, takes him and Sonia too into her house, lavishes expensive gifts on him, and commits serious indiscretions. Mrs. Prettyman, Bertha, and Thomas all protest, but in vain, and she turns out Mrs. Prettyman, who becomes housekeeper to Sir Graham. During the height of her madness Louise has left, in an easily accessible place, not only the diaries recording her past with Sir Graham but also an unpublished novel about which she has been foolish enough to tell Stephen. She goes away with Stephen, leaving Sonia alone in the house, and returns to find all these documents missing. Cured by now of her passion, she is able to see Stephen for what he is—a fraud and a thief. Or rather, Sonia is the thief, since she was given the opportunity to remove the papers. Sonia and Stephen deny all knowledge of the theft and blame the neighbour, Mr. Dooley. This faint niggle of doubt puts Louise in a difficult position. She takes steps to ensure that Stephen does not present *her* unpublished novel as his own, and then awaits developments. They are not long in coming. She learns that Sir Graham Reeves has received an anonymous letter threatening to expose a past indiscretion of his. The chances are overwhelmingly that the writer of the letter has obtained access to the missing diaries and derived his information from them. No money is demanded, however, and the writer's intentions remain unclear. The anonymous letter is couched in such a way that Sir Graham might well suspect Louise herself of having written it. Will he accuse her, thus causing her great pain and distress, possibly even upsetting her mental balance again? Will he—very melodramatic this— take steps to silence her so as to save his own career? Get somebody to bump her off, in fact. If she is out of the way then Stephen can with impunity produce her book, suitably doctored, as his own. And that is his main aim. Sir Graham is really a side issue in Stephen's eyes. What he craves is public acclaim as a writer and he'll stick at nothing to get it.' What's the matter, Brent? I'm sorry if I'm going too fast. I'm afraid I got rather carried away with my story."

I glanced up at him. He had given up all pretence of writing. He was gripping the ball-point pen with both hands as if about to break it in half and he was staring at me with a look of concentrated hatred such as I could not remember seeing on a human face before. It gave me a slight shock but did not for one moment alter my determination.

"And what happens next?" he asked.

"I don't really know," was my reply. "I think perhaps it is for you to say, since Stephen has rather taken over the plot now, hasn't he? It will be interesting to see whether he is capable of bringing it to a conclusion."

"You bitch!" he yelled, and the next moment his hands were at my throat. I managed to ward him off while I said:

"Miss Gray is upstairs—listening. If there's any trouble she'll ring the police."

He flung away and then cried: "You're very pleased with yourself, aren't you, thinking up a trap like this. But it's not original, you know. Other people have used the idea—including Shakespeare in *Hamlet*. I don't know what you think you'll get out of it."

"A Claudius-like admission of guilt, for one thing," I replied. "Thank you for providing me with that."

He swore at me again and then my plan—which had been to insult him and frighten him and work on his feelings until he lost his head completely and dropped some hint as to the whereabouts of the diaries—my plan, as so often happens, was diverted by a totally unexpected incident.

The telephone rang. Very stupidly I had not allowed for this very likely contingency. I let it ring twice. Marian would hear it. There was no extension in the guest room where she was sitting, but there was in my own bedroom next door. Perhaps she would answer it. The ring came again. Brent took a step towards it; it was quite normal for him to take calls for me. But not in his present condition. I had no alternative but to forestall him and pick up the receiver myself.

"Yes?" I said curtly.

"Miss Mitchell?" said a woman's voice, very brisk and official.

"Speaking," I snapped.

"Lord Walters for you. Hold the line, please."

It was too sudden, too emotionally charged. Accustomed

though I was to rapid improvisation, there was nothing I could do to avoid the call.

"Helen? Is that you?"

His voice was very strained; I could feel his effort to breathe.

"Yes," I replied more gently than before. "Helen Mitchell speaking."

My mind was working frantically; this could mean only one thing. How could I reassure him, with Brent standing there taking in every word? Could I make the conversation serve a double purpose, turn it to my own account too?

"Helen—I've had another. You know what I mean. It's just come."

He sounded very bad. His heart must be much worse than he had admitted. And this sort of shock didn't help. I felt weak with loving tenderness.

"Is it on similar lines?" I asked. "Or more specific?"

"Much more specific. A deadline given. Three days. And a large sum mentioned."

I could not reply.

"Helen!" he cried sharply. "Are you there?"

"Yes, Barry. I'm here."

"Did you—could you—how could you—" he gasped and then, making a tremendous effort: "I can't believe it."

"Listen," I said firmly, glancing up at Brent as I did so to make quite sure that he heard, "listen. This wasn't from me. Not this one. But I've found out who was responsible. The leak came through my carelessness and I'm handling it. Will you trust me? I am going to silence the person who is threatening you *even if I have to commit murder to do it*—do you understand?"

I heard Brent gasp—he was standing near me gripping the back of a chair—and I heard Barry gasp too: "Helen—are you mad?"

"If anyone harms you I'll murder them," I repeated. "I mean it. You'll be all right, Barry. I promise you solemnly. Have the amount ready, but do nothing at all until you hear from me. I must go now. I'll let you know when all's well."

I put down the receiver. Brent was staring at me as if I had indeed gone out of my mind.

"You know who that was?" I said very clearly. "Of course you do. Sir Graham in the story—Lord Walters—Barry—in real life. And I meant exactly what I said. If you or Jean send him any more blackmail letters, or if either of you leak out anything whatever to his disadvantage, then I will get you, both of you. You won't escape."

He laughed harshly, but not entirely confidently.

"And how do you propose to carry out this threat? It's not so easy to dispose of people. Look at the hash Hamlet made of it."

"You seem to forget," I replied quietly, "that I have spent a great deal of time and thought on working out ways of killing people off in my books. In addition I have the advantage of having no psychological inhibitions and of not caring what happens to myself. If taking your life were to cost me my own I still would not care."

"Christ—what heroics!" he cried.

"Nevertheless, it happens to be true."

"The woman's mad—yes, she really is stark, staring," he exclaimed with an attempt at casualness, but I noticed that he was backing away towards the door as he spoke.

"You've been warned," I said.

"Excuse me," he said when he had got to the door, "but I don't feel this is quite the moment for sitting down to the typewriter, do you?"

And he was out of the room and down the stairs and out of the house in a flash. At the same moment Marian came stampeding down from the floor above.

"What on earth—?" she began.

"Ssh." I put a finger to my lips. "I want to see what he does."

We moved quickly to the balcony and looked over. Brent raced down the area steps and a few minutes later emerged dragging Jean by the wrist. She seemed to be protesting, but he was determined. They ran across the gardens, nearly knocking down Mr. Thorburn who was returning from his morning walk, to where my car was temporarily parked at the side of the promenade. Brent pushed Jean in and then got in himself and set off with a great roaring of the engine.

"Where are they going?" Marian wanted to know.

''I haven't the slightest idea. The main thing is that they've thoroughly got the wind up and that's what I wanted.''

She bombarded me with questions and I had speedily to invent an acceptable account of the talk with Brent for her consumption. And then simultaneously we both had the same idea: we've got the key—let's search their flat.

15

The flat was tolerably tidy and our recent activities upstairs had made us adept in the art of searching. Marian took the kitchen and bedroom and I took the living-room and the little room that Brent used as a study. We had picked up a nice little walnut desk while furnishing the flat and I pulled open each drawer of this in turn. My heart quickened when I saw a folder containing typed sheets, but it was only the two chapters of his book that he had shown me, followed by a few notes scribbled in his handwriting. In another drawer lay the publisher's setting copy of *Road Without End*, a folder of reviews and congratulatory letters and another of general correspondence. I flicked through this. There were letters from publishers, agents, editors, all bringing the same relentless message: we have read your script and we are very sorry but . . . And underneath, all jumbled together, as if their owner could endure neither to read them again nor to throw them away, was a pile of the rejected scripts.

And these, along with the copies of *Road Without End* on the bookcase, were the only signs of Brent in his capacity as author. Even the novel I had suggested and that had been started with such a flourish had never got beyond those first few chapters. The rest was pretence. He simply had not got it in him. But he could not stop hoping. That one tantalizing little shot of fame had given him such a taste for the stuff that like a heroin addict he would stop at nothing to obtain another dose. No wonder he hated me so much. And hated Barry too, and all successful men and women.

There is always something of pathos about a living home from which the occupants are temporarily absent. The clothes, books, cups and saucers and other small items in constant use have almost the look of amputated parts, so strongly do they hold the impression of the flesh and blood that recently held them. Even the furniture seems to retain something of the warmth of human forms, and letters and papers are yet more moving, containing as they do the impress of the human heart and mind. In this particular case it was a sadly frustrated and tormented mind.

I stifled the upsurge of pity. Brent was threatening Barry, and to protect Barry was my sole object now.

"There's nothing here," I called out to Marian. "How about you?"

"Come and look at this," she replied in tones of suppressed excitement.

I followed her back into the bedroom. She pulled open the doors of the big fitted cupboard with a dramatic gesture. It was crammed with clothes, mostly very expensive-looking and scarcely worn. And on the dressing-table some pieces of jewellery were lying half in and half out of a box, presumably left there by Jean when Brent had torn her away.

Marian surveyed my amazement with satisfaction. "Genuine article," she said. "Diamonds and rubies—where d'you imagine she picked up that little lot?"

"Perhaps Brent bought them for her in his heyday," I said, but not believing it.

"Or she inherited them," said Marian with equal scepticism.

"Or pinched them. Or else she's been operating as a high-class prostitute on the side."

It was all very fascinating, but not what we were searching for.

"Come on," I said, "we don't want to be caught gloating over Jean's diamonds. Was there anything in the kitchen?"

"Only some very pricy Scandinavian ovenware. Nothing cheap to be seen—except her taste in literature."

Marian made an expressive face.

"Not your line at all, Nell. *True Romance. Confessions of*

a Call-Girl. I never knew such stuff existed. There's a whole
row of them alongside the cook-books.''

"There's a big market for it," I said. "I wonder she hasn't
put Brent on to writing it. But perhaps he's no good at that
either.''

We shut the front door and made our way up the area steps.

"Well, what's the verdict?" asked Marian. "Have they got
your scripts? Or are we barking up the wrong tree?''

"I believe they've got them stashed away somewhere—
possibly with a friend or relative of Jean's, and that he has
had such a fright that he has gone to fetch them now. But
there's nothing more we can do until they get back.''

Marian yawned. "I don't know about you, but I'm hun-
gry," she said. "Let's have a quick cold lunch.''

We relaxed over coffee and sandwiches and switched on
the television for the news. One item in particular caught my
attention:

"A letter-bomb was received at the offices of a firm in
Manchester this morning. It is being handled by experts . . .''

Letter-bombs. That scare seemed to be dying out. This
was the first for some weeks.

Letter-bomb! It was a possibility that had not occurred to
me before. Notwithstanding my remarks to Brent I did not,
in fact, intend to go to the trouble of setting up a complicated
lethal booby-trap of the kind that sometimes featured in my
books. I had thought no further, at this stage, than the possibility of threatening him with firearms. Hence my visit to
Philip. He had a licence and a gun—Dora's pressure again.
They liked to think of themselves as landed gentry and they
did in fact occasionally shoot a rabbit in the rough ground
that they called their estate. I would find some way to carry
out my own little theft and by the time it was discovered my
task would be completed. Either I would have extracted both
the papers and the truth from Brent, together with an under-
taking to keep quiet about Barry, or else Brent and Jean and
I would all be beyond human retribution. Three days, Barry
had said; this would give me time enough.

But as I watched the television news my mind began to
work along other lines. A letter-bomb. How neatly that would
fit in to a plot of the kind that Brent and I were working
through together. A bomb in an envelope with the imprint of

a publisher or a literary agent—an irresistible temptation to
Brent to rip it open at once. That would be poetic justice
indeed—the craving that had led him into theft and blackmail
bringing about his own undoing. If I had been writing a book
I should have been delighted with this inspiration. It would
need a lot of research, though; it was a messy and uncertain
way of attacking someone.

I tried to put the idea aside but my mind could not leave
it alone. The newsreader droned on about the latest interna-
tional squabble. And then suddenly I was attentive again: I
had heard a familiar name.

"The rumour that Lord Walters was about to retire owing
to ill health has been strenuously denied. He is in the best of
health and spirits and an important statement concerning the
future of the People's Park may be expected from him early
next week . . ."

I looked up and caught Marian's eye. We smiled at each
other, rather uncertainly. It was evident that she suspected
nothing of his part in my present situation.

"I'm sorry, Nell," she said. "I was a little hasty about
Barry. You know I didn't really mean it."

"Of course I know. And I didn't mean it either. Let's forget him. This letter-bomb business. It's rather fascinating. It's
just occurred to me that it might be convenient to use one in
a novel. No doubt every crime writer on the register has got
the same idea, but never mind. Could any ordinary person
make one, Marian?"

She began to explain in detail—good, unsuspecting, practical old Marian, giving me a demonstration with an actual
envelope and some sugar as if she was explaining to a class
of youngsters. She could scarcely ever have had a more attentive pupil.

"You could fix the explosive like this, with Sellotape,"
she said, "and if you pad out the rest of the envelope it will
simply feel like part of the contents. There are plenty of
explosives—fertilizers, for instance."

It so happened that I had recently made a note of the brand
name of a highly recommended fertilizer for my pot plants
and window boxes. I mentioned it now, speaking as casually
as I could: "That sort of thing, for instance?"

"Yes, that would be ammonium nitrate. Or you could use

sodium chlorate—that's a weedkiller. And sulphur powder—
chemists have that, and finely divided carbon—soot or char-
coal. The explosive is easy enough. It's igniting it that's the
problem. You could keep the two components apart—say by
a strip of polythene, and when the envelope is ripped open
the strip is removed and they come together and react in an
explosion. But in that case one of them would probably have
to be a liquid and that might be tiresome. No, I think it would
be better to use the Christmas cracker principle—where the
spark is generated by the rubbing of a sandpaper surface.''

''Like this?''

I picked up another envelope and set to work with the
Sellotape, deliberately making my actions awkward.

Marian took it from me, saying in friendly contempt:

''I'll finish it. You never were much good at practical
things, Nell.''

I agreed humbly, but as I watched her I knew I could have
made at least as good a job of it as she was making. Marian
was not the only person with whom I found it tactful to assume a high degree of manual non-dexterity. To write best-
sellers and also to be rather clever at making things—this was
too much for some people to swallow, and the latter ability
was much easier to conceal than the former. In any case,
conducting little practical experiments with gas-ovens or
electric fires or invisible wires stretched across staircases is
not everybody's cup of tea, and up to this moment I had never
involved anybody else in this sort of thing.

''There,'' said Marian at last. ''That's not bad for a first
effort, is it?''

''It's terrific,'' I replied. ''And I didn't mean you to go to
all this trouble. It hasn't actually got to *work*—just to sound
convincing in fiction. It's very good of you. Thanks, Marian.
Thanks very much indeed. I suppose you wouldn't like an
official post as scientific adviser to Helen Mitchell, novelist,
would you?''

''I'd have helped you before,'' she said, ''willingly, if you'd
ever asked me. But you always seemed so keen to keep your
writing entirely to yourself.''

It was true. I could see it now, as I could see so many
things. I had kept everyone at a distance; I had drawn the
prison walls around myself, refusing all lesser human rela-

tionships because the most important one of all was denied
to me. And now that I could at last see the way to a wiser
and better life it was too late to take it.

We washed up the few things we had used and then I persuaded Marian to go, telling her that I could see she was
dying to get home to her dark-room, and I was dying to write,
and I would let her know immediately Brent and Jean returned.

"I've a little shopping to do," I said. "We'll start out
together."

At the corner of the terrace we said goodbye and went our
separate ways. The chemist and the garden shop were a few
steps past the newsagent. What a distance it had seemed in
the days when my anxieties had not yet recognized their true
object! And how totally unimportant it was now, this little
walk to the shops. The whole excursion took only ten minutes
and there was still no sign of Brent and Jean when I returned.
I hunted among my stock of stationery, including the big used
envelopes that so often came in handy for packing or for
keeping newspaper cuttings, and I was lucky enough to find
one with my own publisher's imprint. There was no typing
on it and it looked clean and uncrumpled. It had probably
held some small item—a photograph perhaps—that was to be
kept separate inside a larger package. A find indeed.

I put it in the typewriter and addressed it to Brent, taking
great care to make the typing look professional and avoiding
my tendency to run too near the bottom. And then I set to
work on the heart of the matter. All the time my fingers were
busy I was mentally describing what I was doing and explaining to myself why it was necessary to attack Brent in this
way. I mouthed the words: perhaps I even spoke them aloud.
And I referred to myself in the third person: "Never for one
moment did her resolution fail . . ." And so on.

But in fact my resolution was in great danger of failing
when I began to visualize that my action could result in in-
jury, if not death, to another human being, and the only way
I could keep going with my task was to blur the outlines
between fact and fantasy, deliberately pretending that this was
an experiment being carried out for the purposes of writing
a convincing story.

The accused pleads diminished responsibility; the act was

committed while under the influence of the creative imagination . . .

Had anybody ever put forward such a plea in a court of law? It was as valid an excuse as any. Fantasy carried to excess can deaden the senses in the same way as drink or drugs, can produce a complete detachment from one's surroundings. The fantastic imagination is a powerful, frightening faculty of the human mind; kept to its place, it is a useful safety valve; allowed out of its place . . .

I finished my task and stared at the horrible booby-trap that I had made. Was it a safety valve or was I going to use it? And what, if I used it successfully on Brent, was I going to do about Jean? Must she be the next victim? Could I not keep them both quiet by threats alone? Should I offer them money? Or do a deal with Brent—books to be published under his name in exchange for his leaving Barry in peace. Not just the two books he had taken, but more and more, all the words that my restless mind could produce. If I made such a bargain then nobody need be hurt; there would be no blood and mangled flesh outside the printed page, and how gladly I would climb back on to the treadmill again when I knew I was doing it all for the sake of the man I loved.

I placed the explosive envelope on the table, well away from the rest of the correspondence, settled myself in a chair by the window and remained there deep in thought. The sky was darkening and there was still no sign of Brent's return. He had been gone for hours—time to get up to London and back. My mind turned to his own friends and relatives. There was a brother in Croydon and one or two friends whom he occasionally mentioned. Perhaps one of them, and not an acquaintance of Jean's, was holding the missing documents.

I was very exhausted. Barry's visit, the sleepless night, the quarrel with Brent, the searching his flat, the making of the envelope—all this hectic activity had taken its toll. I dozed with my eyes open, staring at the horizon, the radio gently burbling soft music at my side.

Then suddenly I was alert: the music had given way to the synthetic voice of the announcer:

". . . of a heart attack early this afternoon at his country home, only a short while after rumours of his ill-health had been denied. Lord Walters was fifty-six. There will be an

extended obituary in our next news-bulletin, including appre-
ciations recorded by the Prime Minister, the Leader of the
Opposition, and . . .''

I switched off the radio and sat motionless for some while.
Then I rose and turned on the lights and drew the curtains
and puffed up the cushions and performed many other little
actions like an automaton until the mechanism of reasoning
began again. The envelope—it would not be needed now. I
had made it to protect Barry, and now Barry was dead, dead,
dead.

But I must not think of Barry now. I must concentrate on
the job in hand—to get rid of the letter. But how? The only
thing about an amateur letter-bomb that I had omitted to learn
was how to render it harmless, and I had not the will to
experiment with a dummy. Should I phone Marian? Should I
try to dispose of it in some other way—fling it out to sea from
the end of the pier, perhaps?

I stood by the side of the table, my fingers resting lightly
on the bulky manilla envelope. I was stunned, barely conscious; it was impossible to come to any decision, to take
any action.

In this state of failing senses I did not hear Brent come
in—neither the car drawing up nor his footsteps on the stairs.
I became aware of him only when I heard his voice, not
particularly friendly, but tolerably self-controlled.

''I've been thinking things over, Helen—''

He broke off as he caught sight of the envelope.

''Christ!'' he exclaimed in sudden fury, ''she's nicking my
letters now!''

He stretched out a hand—he had seen his name and the
publisher's imprint and ecstatic fantasies had instantly taken
possession of his mind. He had not seen that the stamp bore
no postmark.

I grabbed the letter and held it with both hands, backing
away from him and shaking my head violently.

''It's a fake!'' I cried. ''It's a bomb. Keep away—keep
away!''

He made a loud noise of disgust and leapt towards me,
snatching at the top of the envelope; my hands still gripped
the sides.

''Let *go*!'' I screamed. ''It's a bomb! I meant it for you.''

He swore at me, still pulling at the stiff paper, and then laughed, opening his mouth wide and miming a vomit.

"You! You only spew out words. You never *act*!"

"But this time, I did. It's *true*!"

I saw doubt dawning in his eyes. Had I let go then he would have examined the envelope carefully before tearing it open and would have realized the truth. And had his fingers relaxed ever so slightly, then mine would have done so too. We wanted to abandon the struggle, both of us, but our muscles would not obey our wills. The tension was too great between us.

The paper gave at last. The makeshift ignition of taped-together sandpaper did its work only too well. The noise and the heat and the smell seemed to last an eternity and I saw Brent's face, and my own face in the mirror, before I saw and heard no more.

16

There was a blinding light and oceans of pain. Time passed and then the light and pain returned. Then the light flickered and became very dim; the storms of pain died down to a strong tide below the surface, and there were many little noises. One of the sounds was my own groaning. More time passed and I came back to consciousness to see a freckled face surmounted by ginger hair under a white cap.

"Dora," I murmured, wondering why it was I who was lying in bed when it was Phil who had been wounded.

"I'm Nurse Arthur," said the face. "Are you feeling more comfortable now?"

I explored before replying. The legs and one arm were mobile but an arm and one eye and much of the head was bandaged.

"What—how much—my eye?" I muttered.

"It will be all right," she soothed. "You'll have a lot of the vision back. And your arm is only burns. They'll heal up."

"Anyone else . . ."

It was all I could manage to say; my mouth felt as if it had been rubbed with sandpaper.

"Burns on the arm," replied the nurse, quickly interpreting my enquiry. "Not as bad as yours. He was treated and allowed to go home."

I felt a few tears of relief ooze out from my uncovered eye: I could say no more.

157

"Try not to worry, try to save your breath," said the nurse. "I'll call your brother. He's been waiting hours for you to come round."

Philip looked scared and strained as he bent close to ask in a low voice how I was feeling.

"Apparently I shall survive," I tried to move my lips in a smile but the pain was excruciating. "Tell Dora," I gasped, "tell Dora she won't inherit yet."

His face twisted up as if he too was about to weep.

"Don't say that, Nell," he begged. "We don't need your money. And I'd much rather you were alive."

"I'm sorry," I replied. And then, when I felt able to speak again: "Barry's dead, Phil."

"Yes. Yesterday afternoon. There were long news items on the television and radio, and today's papers are full of him. Would you like to see them? You won't be able to read much yourself, but I will read the obituaries to you if you would like me to."

It was said very kindly and I thanked him with as much warmth as my charred mouth could muster.

"Tomorrow," I said. "I'm too tired now. Were they—were they good notices, Phil?"

"Very good indeed. Not a dissentient voice."

I sighed. "He'd have liked that. I wonder what notices I shall get when I die."

"You're not dead yet," said Philip, more firmly this time. "You'll be up and about and out of hospital and scribbling away again in a very few weeks' time. Though I sincerely trust you won't carry your passion for accuracy in your novels to the extent of another experiment with explosives."

"Experimenting with explosives?" I repeated slowly. "Was that what I was doing?"

"Apparently," said Philip, and he was just about to enlarge on the subject when the nurse returned and said that was quite enough for the moment and I must have another injection. He had said enough, however, to start me thinking, and when I awoke from a long sleep, refreshed and with a clearer mind, I decided not to offer any explanation of how the accident had come about until I had heard what was being said—in other words, what was Brent's version.

"Was I concussed?" I asked Philip when he came again.

"I can't seem to remember anything at all. Marian was staying with me and she'd gone off to a dinner—oh no, she'd gone home to do some photographic developing, that's right. And I was expecting Brent to come and talk over some scheme we had. But after that it's all confused."

"I'm not surprised," said Philip, "and you're incredibly lucky that you weren't more seriously injured, the pair of you."

"But what happened? Doesn't Brent remember either?"

"Your 'scheme'," said Philip, disapproval breaking into his voice in spite of his attempt to be kind and patient, "was to test whether it was possible to make an effective letter-bomb, using easily available household materials and with no more equipment than that found in an ordinary house. Of all the damn' silly notions!"

He controlled himself and went on:

"I quite appreciate that a certain amount of personal research is necessary for the purposes of artistic verisimilitude, but to take it to such lengths is positively imbecilic. If you and Brent Ashwood wanted to introduce letter-bombs into your new novel then why on earth couldn't you obtain the information you wanted from expert sources?"

I let Philip do his bit of scolding. After all, he had had a very nasty shock himself over me, and he was staying in Brighton to attend to all my affairs at considerable inconvenience to himself. But my main reason for not interrupting him was my amazement at the story that Brent had told. It had not for a moment occurred to me that he would tell anything but the truth. I had assumed that he would be delighted to accuse me, and that when I recovered I should face all sorts of unpleasant charges and that it would be something of a miracle if Philip succeeded in keeping me out of gaol.

It was therefore with feelings of relief mixed with suspicion that I learned Brent's version of the affair. We were planning a book together—he and I—a statement given credence by the earlier rumour about our collaboration—and a tussle over a letter-bomb was the climax of the plot. We had decided to make a convincing-looking dummy and also a "real" bomb. The former would serve to test out what would happen to the envelope in the struggle; the latter would serve to discover how easy it was to make. I, apparently, had insisted on

procuring the materials and doing most of the work and there
had been a little argument about it because he didn't feel he
had taken his full share.

At that point I interrupted Phil.

"It's coming back," I said. "I asked Marian about it.
Didn't I ask Marian? She must remember. What does she
say?"

I awaited his reply with great anxiety. What had Marian
said indeed; had she blown the gaffe? Revealed the tension
between Brent and myself? Or did her story tie in with his?

"She says you were asking her about making letter-
bombs," said Philip, "in order to use the idea in a story. But
she didn't realize it was to be in collaboration with Brent.
She says she finds that difficult to believe. I can't understand
it either. Why are you joining forces with him, Nell? You
don't really need a co-author, do you?"

"It's a long story," I said. "Too long to explain now. But
I have my reasons. Marian didn't know that Brent and I were
doing the book together. I thought she wouldn't help me if
she knew. As you say, she doesn't like Brent much. But I still
don't understand exactly what happened. It's coming back
slowly—the dummy, the real thing—but how did it go off?"

"You mistook the envelopes, so Ashwood says. Picked up
the explosive one instead of the dummy and realized too late.
He managed to get it a little distance away—otherwise it
would have been full in your face."

"The room must be in a mess," I said.

"It is rather," he replied. "There's quite a lot of china
gone, but the desk is all right."

"And the envelope—the letter-bomb itself?"

"That was pretty well shredded, but the dummy was in-
tact. Padded out with sugar. Very ingenious."

I fetched up a deep sigh. "I'm terribly muddled," I said.
"I don't know how I am going to make a statement for the
police."

In fact my confusion was by no means all assumed, and it
was not until Brent came to see me that the picture became
clear. His left arm was in a sling and there were burn marks
on his face but otherwise he looked much as usual.

"Poor old Helen." He put a large basket of fruit on my
bedside table. "I'm afraid you got the worst of it."

"Yes," I replied. "I never did like pulling Christmas crackers and this was a particularly nasty one."

"It sure was. Might well have been fatal to one of us. How lucky that we managed to share it."

His voice was friendly enough but I sensed menace behind everything he said. I shuddered inwardly but at the same time was conscious of an extraordinary feeling of repose. This man now had me completely in his power—he knew my past, he knew my present. He knew that I had set up a trap to kill or injure him and he knew my motive. If he cared to, he could turn the biographer's spotlight upon me, searching out every little cranny, leaving nothing sacred. How strange that this man whom I disliked and despised should know me even better than Barry had known me! Or perhaps it was not so strange; perhaps only our enemies can really know us; our friends we must always deceive because we care what they think of us.

Now that I had nothing more to hide from Brent I could relax completely.

"Yes," I replied. "You'd have got a horrible blast if you'd torn open that letter as you wanted to. But I did try to stop you—remember? I think I deserve some credit, even if it is fair retribution that I should get the lion's share."

The nurse came in at that moment and we all made suitable noises at each other. When she had gone Brent said:

"I under-estimated you. I thought you would never really do anything."

"I wouldn't have done anything if you hadn't turned up at that moment. In fact I was still very undecided about it even before I heard on the radio that Barry was dead."

"Nevertheless," he said severely, sounding for a moment not unlike my brother, "you made the bomb and it was clearly addressed to me. I don't know what further evidence is required of intent to murder."

"This question of intent," I said, "is always rather tricky, both in literature and in law. Sometimes evil intentions do less harm than good ones. We all know what the path to hell is paved with."

"I wouldn't know about good intentions," he replied. "Probably I've never had any. Maybe I'm going to hell all the same but it doesn't worry me much. Where I'm going in

this world—that's all I care about. However, we'd better not
talk about it just yet. Wait till you're up and about again.''

I agreed that I was too tired to talk business and he asked
if my eye was very sore.

"Funny thing," he added, "you read and write about explosives but you don't realize quite how much it hurts.''

For some minutes we exchanged symptoms in an amicable
manner and then he enquired most solicitously about my re-
quirements in the way of books, crossword puzzles, and so
on.

I explained that Philip had been attending to such matters.

"Bit hard on him, isn't it?" said Brent. "Having to cope
with all this.''

I agreed unhappily, feeling a return of the tears that were
never very far away but that had been so strangely absent
during the conversation with Brent. There was, after all, no
escape from pangs of conscience.

"Please Brent," I began, and had to stop and gulp a little
before I could go on.

"Yes, ma'am?"

He assumed a respectful and attentive attitude.

"Please be nice to Phil," I said weakly. "None of this
mess is his fault.''

"I am very nice to Philip," was the reply. "Very dutiful,
very co-operative, very grateful. It is bad policy to quarrel
with one's solicitor.''

He looked down at me and shook his head.

"Poor old Helen. You really are in a bad way. It's not like
you to be so maudlin. Never mind. You'll soon get over it
and be sharpening up your claws again.''

I was relieved when he went and yet already looking forward to his coming again. Meanwhile there was Marian's visit
to be endured. I managed with great difficulty to convince
her that I had not been conspiring with Brent behind her back
to make a fool of her and then I tried to make her understand
just how unpleasant he could make things for me. She continued to argue. If Brent accused me of attempting to bomb
him then I should bring a counter-accusation for the theft of
my manuscripts.

"Get the whole thing out into the open," she said with a

sort of virtuous relish. "There's been far too much concealment all round."

She could see herself in the witness-box, the steady, upright representative of common sense and scientific truth to
whom judge, jury and counsel alike would turn to rest their
tired brains after hearing all the wild and fantastic tales that
these crazy writers had to tell.

"It's no good," I said. "There are other reasons why I
have to keep quiet. You don't know the half of it."

She looked hurt then, as well she might, at this phrase
uttered so thoughtlessly which was yet equivalent to banging
the door in her face. I tried a half-explanation which was
perhaps worse than none at all.

"I think Brent has also got some old letters of mine that
were in the drawer with the typescripts," I said. "Nothing
very dreadful in themselves, but I'd rather their contents were
not made public all the same."

She made a sound of disgust. "Barry, I suppose."

I did not contradict her.

"He's dead," I reminded her quietly.

"Yes," she retorted, "and now you've found another man
to grovel around and make yourself into a doormat for. You
really are hopeless, Nell."

I could not reply. She had hit the nail firmly on the head.
It served me right for sneering at her passion for scientific
truth.

"Why can't you just be yourself?" she went on. "Surely
you've got brains and talent and personality enough. Do you
have to spend your whole life submerging your identity in
your characters or defining your identity in terms of somebody else?"

I tried to tease her. "You've been reading the sociologists.
You're picking up the jargon."

She waved this aside impatiently. "It's depressing enough,
God knows, in those wretched little mousy wives who have
to ask *him* which way they should vote or what newspaper they
should read. But when it comes to a woman like yourself—"

For a moment words failed her.

"And he hasn't even got Barry's ability, this odious creature," she said.

"I wouldn't be so sure of that," I replied. "I was inclined

to underrate him at first myself but he has definitely got the potential and he only needs the appropriate circumstances to call it out. I would say that he has a great gift for seizing an opportunity and making the most of it. Yes, I think on the whole he is developing very well.''

Marian stared at me for some seconds before she spoke.

"I don't know whether you are serious or not. If you are joking, then it's in very bad taste. And yet I cannot believe even of you that you seriously intend to encourage this horrible young man in a life of fraud and blackmail and even worse.''

"I don't know what I am going to do," I said, falling back against the pillows and hoping that Marian would take this as a hint to depart. But she was well launched on one of her crescendoes of indignation and there was no stopping her until she had passed the peak.

"I know exactly what you are going to do!" she cried, and even pointed an accusing finger at me. "You're going to do what you never managed to with Barry—you're going to *marry* Brent in order to build up his career. Oh yes—" she waved aside my feeble protests—"I know you pretended you wanted to get rid of him—dragging me through all that farce of trying to catch him out—"

"I did want.to get rid of him," I cried, "and I did need your help!"

She went on as if I had not spoken:

"—and all the time you were double-crossing me, working at this book on which you were to collaborate with him. Collaborate!" She gave an expressive snort. "We know what that means. You'll be writing his books for him next—just as you used to write Barry's speeches.''

"Oh no," I murmured, and held my hand over my face. "I can't do that, Marian. Even I couldn't sink quite so low as that.''

"There's no knowing how far you may sink," she said gloomily. "Oh well, I suppose I'll have to hang around again to pick up the pieces.''

She moved to the door.

"There's just one more thing, Nell. Do please take care. This man is dangerous. That's where he differs from Barry. Barry would bankrupt you or ruin your career or murder your character without turning a hair. But he would never actually get his hands round your throat or put poison in your coffee. This man would. If you've absolutely got to marry him, then for God's sake make sure it's in his own interests to keep you alive.''

I dropped my hand from my face and stared at her, making no attempt to hide my own horrified awareness of what my future might be.

''But there's only one way to do that,'' I said.

EPILOGUE

I can write no more. He has guessed that I am deceiving
him. That book I am supposed to be writing for him makes
little progress, for all my creative gifts are poured out into
these anxious secret sessions. This one must be the last.
Marian's visits will serve as an excuse no longer. He was in
any case very reluctant to let her come, but I told him that
I would never regain the health and spirits to write at all if
I could not sometimes have the comfort of a visit from an
old friend. The argument carried weight, for I am of no use
to him if I cannot write. Besides, he dislikes leaving me
here alone, but he cannot always act as jailer and he himself
longs to escape from the tense atmosphere of this beautiful
doom-laden house and relax with younger and less critical
female company.

I don't care in the least how many girls he picks up as long
as I don't have to receive them, although oddly enough I was
sorry to see Jean go. She gave up her job and looked after
me when I was convalescing from the accident and, evidently
regarding me now as morally on a par with herself, she chat-
ted to me quite freely about all the gentlemen who had given
her lovely presents. She kept house beautifully—even better
than my dear Mrs. Simmonds—and we had some very amicable conversations about antique jewellery, which was one
of the two ruling passions of her life. The other was Brent,
and our marriage was more than she could swallow. She

167

moved out, leaving me feeling a trifle guilty, although in fact
I believe he still sees her.

Marian does not know what I am writing. She thinks it
is only solitude for which I crave—the chance to sit quietly
in my lovely room and dream that it belongs once more to
me. She takes herself down to Mrs. Simmonds's old flat as
soon as Brent has left the house, and reads and watches
television there, keeping a look-out for his return. When
he gets back she is sitting upstairs with me, idly chatting;
but she has in her capacious handbag a few letters of mine
to post, including a large manilla envelope addressed to
Philip.

"It's some old articles of our father's," I tell her. "I'm
gradually sorting them out and sending them to him. You
remember that box of papers we came across when we were
hunting through the house? It's not that I'm trying to hide
anything from Brent, but I do get rather a lot of cross-
examination whenever I write to Philip, so if you don't
mind—"

Brent, of course, suspects that I am deliberately writing a
poorer quality type of novel to appear under his name. He
tinkers about with my first draft for hours on end, partly to
persuade himself that he really is taking part in the authorship
for which he intends to claim full credit, and partly to try to
discover just where the weakness of the novel lies. I help him
a little to gain time and keep him quiet while I finish my own
story and make up my mind what to do. His hate and frustration could drive him to kill me. He knows it could, and
that is why he holds on to the two stolen typescripts and
makes no attempt to bully me into revising them so that they
can appear as his own work. They are his insurance policy,
as once they were mine; if he can get away with murder he
will then produce them as his own.

I don't mind what happens to them. I care for nothing
except this "novel" that I have now completed. These last
sheets will go into a long envelope that will be sealed and
placed inside the one addressed to Philip. On it will be written: "To be deposited with my will and opened after my
decease."

Philip thinks it is a novel to be published posthumously.
Perhaps that is just what it is. On one of the rare occasions

when I was able to talk to him freely I told him that I was
doing it in this way because I wanted it off my mind the
moment it had been written; I didn't want to be tempted to
revise. He may or may not have believed me; we have, of
course, become estranged since my marriage to Brent. Dora
was furious about it, in spite of my assurance that I was
leaving only the house to Brent in my will. If I should die,
he himself can expect no mercy. He will have many enemies.
His life will be as anxious and guilt-ridden as it is now. For
if I am unhappy, he is scarcely less so. We torment each other
in an infinite variety of ways—personal insults, threats of ex-
posure, reminders of past errors; but the picture we present
to the outside world is—amazingly—one of a successful part-
nership. I only wish it were true. There was a time when I
believed I would gladly trade my gift for a renewal of passion;
now I wish even more that it could buy me my freedom and
the chance to lead a quiet and fearless life. But that can never
be. Not while he lives.

And so I end my last story with the question with which I
began: do I set up the death-trap? Not a fumbling attempt
like the letter-bomb this time, but a deadly certainty, a method
that I researched intensively for one of my earlier books and
that cannot fail.

I look out at the luminous evening sea, pale now, merg-
ing imperceptibly into the sky beyond; I hear the hum of
traffic and the screech of gulls and the cries of happy children returning from the beach to the nearby hotel. Life
can be very sweet in spite of all. Who am I to deprive a
fellow creature of his full share of it? I could not live with
such a crime behind me. I can take no action; it is he who
must decide. The plot is his and it is for him alone to end
it.

He will be back any moment now, and when he comes
these folded sheets will be safe in Marian's bag. And when
he accuses me of cheating him and mocking him for his
own lack of inspiration, I shall tell him that I am finished
and can write no more—neither for him nor for myself. I
no longer dread what he will do in his hopeless rage. I
have purged my fear; yet once again I have written it all
away.

But perhaps, after all, justice will be mine, for I shall not tell him about this book. When the moment comes for the final reckoning these last pages will be in the post on their way to Philip, and Philip is a good and clever lawyer and he will know what to do.